Upside Down

Also by Mary Jane Miller

ME AND MY NAME

UPSIDE DOWN

MARY JANE MILLER

VIKING

My special thanks to my editor, Deborah Brodie, for her wise counsel, guidance, encouragement, and loving concern; to my agent, Jane Jordan Browne, for her faith, loving care, generous help, and encouragement. I am grateful to Karen, Tom, and David Boston; Colleen, Don, and Katie Reid; and Mark Cochrane for significant details. I wish to thank Melinda and Leanne for reading day and night with insight and unwavering good cheer. I am especially grateful to Joe for always being there with love and support. I wish to thank the Wednesday group, my sisters-in-the-craft, for their advice, generosity of spirit, and support. A special thank you to Maude. And of course, thank you, Thaddeus and Company.

VIKING
Published by the Penguin Group
Viking Penguin, a division of Penguin Books USA Inc.,
375 Hudson Street, New York, New York 10014, U.S.A.
Penguin Books Ltd, 27 Wrights Lane, London W8 5TZ, England
Penguin Books Australia Ltd, Ringwood, Victoria, Australia
Penguin Books Canada Ltd, 10 Alcorn Avenue, Toronto, Ontario, Canada M4V 3B2
Penguin Books (N.Z.) Ltd, 182–190 Wairau Road, Auckland 10, New Zealand

Penguin Books Ltd, Registered Offices: Harmondsworth, Middlesex, England

First published in 1992 by Viking Penguin, a division of Penguin Books USA Inc.

1   3   5   7   9   10   8   6   4   2

Library of Congress Cataloging-in-Publication Data
Miller, Mary Jane.
Upside down / by Mary Jane Miller.   p.   cm.
Summary: When her mother starts dating the father
of the local nerd, Sara seeks the courage to accept
the inevitable changes in her family and her life.
ISBN 0-670-83648-6 (hardcover)
[1. Mothers and daughters—Fiction. 2. Family life—Fiction.] I. Title.
PZ7.M6312Up   1992   [Fic]—dc20   91-28873   CIP   AC

Printed in U.S.A.   Set in 12 point Century Expanded

In memory of my father, John Arthur,
and for my mother, Ceil,
my brother Bob,
my husband Joe,
and to our ever expanding family circle.
Love always ———————— Always love.

UPSIDE DOWN

CHAPTER ONE

THE MINUTE my brother, Jon, walked into the kitchen, he started yelling at me, "Get off the phone, Sara, you'll be late for school!"

I looked at the clock. It was only seven-thirty. "There's plenty of time. Give me a break." Jon gave me the stare.

"I'm talking to Mollie," I told him. Jon knows that Mollie and I talk every morning. Mollie's my best friend. Jon kept on staring, so I turned my back to him.

"I had the most awful nightmare last night," I said to Mollie. "I dreamt we were in different rooms." Mollie and I have been in the same room since kindergarten, but this year we're going to Maplebrook Junior High. There are three sixth grades at Maplebrook, so Mollie and I have been worrying all summer that we won't be together.

Jon yanked on my ponytail so hard I was sure I'd have a bald spot. And when you have dark brown hair, a bald spot would really show. "Cut it out, Jon."

"Hang up! I mean it. If you're late for school, Mom will have a cow. She doesn't need the hassle. You know that!"

"I've got to go, Mollie. I'll meet you at the corner." I hung up and faced Jon. "Who made you my boss? For your information, I can tell time. And I don't hassle Mom, so leave me alone!"

"Sara, what's going on?" Mom walked into the kitchen frowning.

"Jon's acting like a jerk," I told Mom. I gave Jon a dirty look at the same time. "He thinks he's Dad." As soon as the words popped out of my

2

mouth I wanted to grab them back. "Mom . . . I didn't mean it. I didn't mean Dad was a jerk."

"Oh, Sara," Mom said sadly, "I know that." She rubbed her forehead as if a bad headache was coming on. Mom gets headaches when she's upset.

Jon glared at me. His eyes said, Now look what you've done. It's hard to believe, but Jon used to be fun. But for the past year, Jon's been about as much fun as watching a spider crawl up your arm. Just because he's seventeen, Jon thinks he's the man of the family, my boss. Mr. Karate Kid.

"You better get ready, Sara, or you'll be late," Mom said. And then, as if she were talking to herself, she added, "I wish you wouldn't fight with Jon." Jon didn't say anything.

"I'm sorry," I muttered and ran out of the kitchen. Why can't I keep my mouth shut? I thought, as I climbed the stairs to my room. It's weird the way Jon and I fight. We never used to get into big fights before the accident.

I hate thinking about the accident. It makes me feel cold inside. But sometimes thoughts about it just go round and round in my head. Why do guns have to go off and kill people? Why didn't Daddy listen to Mom? She didn't want him to go hunting.

I sat down on my bed. Patches, my cat, was curled up on my pillow. I buried my face in her soft fur. "I'm not going to cry," I told Patches. I reached over and turned on B96 full blast. The Restless Ones were singing "Walk My Way." If music is loud enough and you sing along with it, you can't hear yourself think.

After I brushed out my ponytail, I put on my black frosted jeans. Mollie and I had decided black jeans would be cool. Then I raced around my room making sure everything was picked up. Last year, before the accident, I could have cared less if my nightshirts, underwear, and socks made friends with the dust puffies under my bed. Now I like everything neat. I've even arranged my books alphabetically by author. Except for my Nancy Drew case files; they're arranged by number.

When I walked back into the kitchen, Jon had left. Mom was sitting at the table drinking tea and reading a fat book. Mom's a librarian; she's always reading. She smiled at me. Whew! I was glad the sad look had disappeared from her face. Mom didn't say anything about the fight. I guess she decided to pretend it didn't happen, which was okay with me.

"Bye, Mom." I plopped a kiss on her cheek. As I started out the door, Mom called after me, "Sara, don't forget to come right home after school. I'm leaving the library early so we'll have plenty of time to get to the dentist."

"Mom! Do we have to? It's the first day of school. Can't we go another day?"

"No," Mom answered firmly. "You're a new patient and today was the first appointment I could get for you. We talked about this yesterday."

"Okay." I didn't want to risk a fight with Mom, especially after what had already happened this morning.

Mollie was waiting for me at the corner. We ran all the way to school, which wasn't too far, only three blocks. "It looks bigger than it did when we were here for orientation last year," Mollie whispered to me when we stopped in front of the two-story brick building.

"Let's find the class lists and pray we have Bradford," I said to Mollie. The sixth-grade class lists were posted on the bulletin board in the foyer. Mollie and I pushed our way up to them.

"All right! Bradford! We have Bradford," Mollie shouted, pointing to her name.

I stared at the class list. "Where's my name?" My name wasn't on Bradford's list.

"You have Pitney!" Mollie cried, with a look of horror on her face.

"Pitney? I can't have Pitney. She teaches eighth grade math."

"Not anymore. Look."

My name, Sara Kovar, stared at me from the middle of Mrs. Pitney's list. If it was possible to grow wings, I would have sprouted a pair and flown right out of Maplebrook Junior High. It wouldn't matter where I landed, anyplace would be better than Pitney's room.

Pitney's mean, hard, and crabby. She hates kids, never smiles, and can't take a joke. Jon said so. He had Pitney for math three years ago. My dad used to say Jon was the thorn in Pitney's side. When Pitney finds out I'm Jon's sister she'll hate me for sure.

"Sara, look. It's worse than awful. Adam Quigley has Pitney, too." Mollie pointed to the class list again.

"Oh no," I groaned. A double whammy. There should be a law somewhere that says two awful things can't happen to you on the same day. How was I going to spend another year in the same room with Adam Quigley—without Mollie?

Adam is the world's biggest dork. Last year, in fifth grade, he chased me around the school yard yelling, "Kovar crunches cooties," zapped my legs with at least twenty thousand rubber bands, and then had the nerve to send me five valentines signed, "Guess who." I knew they were from Adam because he'd put a tiny little *a* on the back of each one.

The bell rang as Mollie and I stared at the class list. "Bradford's in 107 and Pitney's in 119," Mollie said. We found 107 right away. "See you at lunch," she said.

Pitney's room had to be at the end of the hall. It wasn't. Great, just great. I was going to be late.

I started racing down the hall, zigzagging between some kids who looked like they were eighth graders. One of them, a girl with hair that reached her waist, swirled around and said in a stuck-up voice, "Watch where you're going." Then I heard her say, "Look at those jeans." Everybody laughed. I'm never, ever wearing black jeans again.

A tall woman with a poodle perm and owl

glasses was standing outside one of the rooms. She called out, "Stop running, young lady," as I sped by her. I skidded to a stop and turned around. The teacher stared at me with X-ray eyes. "Where are you going?" she asked sharply.

Pitney. I was eyeball to eyeball with Pitney. "Room 119," I squeaked.

Crooking her finger at me, Pitney said, "You just passed room 119. What's your name?"

I thought about making up a name. Sara Thomas. Or Sara Smith. But it wouldn't work. Mrs. Pitney would find out my real name and then I'd be in trouble for lying. I decided to tough it out. I looked Mrs. Pitney right in the eye and said, "Sara Kovar."

Mrs. Pitney's eyebrows went up very slowly. "Any relation to Jon Kovar?"

I was doomed. Mrs. Pitney was probably remembering the time Jon flushed a tennis ball down the boys' toilet. It caused a major flood. Or she was thinking about the time Jon brought straws to school and started a spitball war. Why did Jon have to hit Mrs. Pitney right between the eyes with a spitball? Jon used to make me laugh so hard my stomach would hurt when he told the story. I

8

wasn't laughing now. "He's my brother," I said, looking down at my shoes.

Mrs. Pitney sighed and said, "Go into the room, Sara, and take the seat in the last row." The only empty desk in the last row was the desk next to Adam Quigley. Adam gave me a dorky grin when I sat down. He looked the same as he did last year. Tall and skinny. He even had the same silly spiked hair.

"Catch any cooties this summer, Kovar?" Adam whispered, scratching his head.

I ignored him.

CHAPTER TWO

FIFTEEN MINUTES seems like five hours when you're waiting around in the dentist's office. Especially when it's a new dentist. I missed Dr. McDonald. Why did he have to move to Florida? My teeth belonged to him. Not to some stranger.

"Sara, stop wiggling around," Mom whispered. "Find something to read." There wasn't anything. Newsmagazines are boring. And who wants to read a little kid's book called *I'm Going to the Dentist*?

There was nothing to do but people-watch. Mom says it's impolite to stare, but what else can you do when a woman with a tattoo on her arm is sitting across from you?

Every time I looked away, my eyes would go back to the tattoo. It would freak me out if my mom wore a big red heart on her arm. Just as I started to whisper to Mom, "Look at the tattoo," the nurse called my name.

When I was stretched out on the long black chair, a man with brown hair, bushy eyebrows, and big ears came into the room. "Hi, Sara, I'm Dr. Quigley," he said.

Dr. Quigley? I had seen his name on the sign, but my brain must have been asleep, because I never thought, Adam's father? Don't be stupid, I told myself. He can't be Adam's father. He doesn't look like Adam except for his ears. And anyway, there must be a lot of people named Quigley.

"Anything wrong, Sara? Do you want your mother to come in?"

I shook my head. Great! I probably looked like a goofy little kid who's afraid of the dentist. I hoped my face wasn't turning red.

"Open wide, then," Dr. Quigley ordered. He

poked around my mouth. "Hmm. You have a cavity. Are you a novocaine person?"

What's a novocaine person? What a dorky question. I had an important question to ask. "Do you need a needle for novocaine?" Dr. Quigley nodded. Needles are long and scary. But what if the drill hurts? Some choice. Thinking about being stuck in the mouth with a needle made me shiver, so I decided to take my chances with the drill.

When the drilling started, I stared at the ceiling. It was white with little black specks that reminded me of bugs. Gross! I closed my eyes and tried to think about something besides bugs and the whir of the drill. All I could think about was Adam Quigley. What if Dr. Quigley was Adam's father? He couldn't be. It would be too embarrassing.

"You can open your eyes now," Dr. Quigley said.

"It's over?"

"Yes. It was a small cavity. We caught it just in time."

While I was getting out of the chair, Dr. Quigley asked me how I liked school. Another dumb question. Why do grown-ups think they have to ask you about school? No way was I going to tell him that Mrs. Pitney scared me and I missed being with Mollie. It was none of his business. I gave my shoulders a little shrug and said, "Okay. I guess."

"You're in sixth grade, aren't you?" Dr. Quigley asked, as he wrote on my chart. "So's my son, Adam. He goes to Maplebrook."

"Are you Adam Quigley's father?" I blurted out. Now I was asking a dumb question. Of course he was Adam's father. There was only one Adam Quigley in sixth grade at Maplebrook.

Dr. Quigley smiled at me. "Do you know Adam?"

I nodded. Boy, do I know Adam. And now Adam would know all about me and my teeth. He'd even know I'd drooled on the bib. Tomorrow it would be all over the school. I wanted to say, Don't tell Adam about me. But how can you tell a grown-up what to do?

Dr. Quigley kept on asking me questions. "Do you know my daughter, Laurel? She's in eighth grade." Then he showed me a picture of a girl with hair down to her waist. She looked familiar. Just as I figured out that Laurel Quigley was the snooty girl who laughed at my jeans and told me to watch where I was going this morning, Mom popped her head in the door.

"How's Sara doing?" she asked.

After Dr. Quigley told Mom about my cavity, Mom and Dr. Quigley started to chat. I couldn't believe Mom was talking to Adam's father as if they were friends. I gave Mom a please-let's-go look, but Mom kept right on chatting. I couldn't figure out why Mom was so interested in hearing about Jefferson High School, a twenty-fifth-year reunion, and somebody named Mr. Devitt. It all sounded pretty boring to me. And besides, I didn't want to know anything about Adam's father. Mom had to find us a new dentist. Finally, when I started twirling a strand of my hair around my finger and scraping the floor with the tip of my shoe, Mom got the idea it was time to leave.

At the door, Dr. Quigley gave me a pink eraser shaped like a tooth and said to Mom, "It's been good talking to you, Ellen. Why don't we get together for coffee? I'll give you a call tomorrow."

When Mom said, "I'd like that, David," I dropped the tooth eraser. Why would Mom want to have coffee with Adam's father? She never drinks coffee.

14

While we were walking to the car, I told Mom that Dr. Quigley was Adam's father. "Do I know Adam?" Mom asked.

Sometimes Mom just spaces out. "Adam's the one who's always bugging me. Remember, when you picked me up after school, I told you Mrs. Pitney made me sit next to him."

"Oh." Mom laughed. "That Adam."

That's all Mom said. She didn't seem to mind that our dentist's son drives me bonkers and is the world's biggest dork. And why hadn't Mom told me she knew Dr. Quigley? "How do you know Adam's father?" I asked.

Mom smiled. "Dr. Quigley and I went to the same high school. We had Mr. Devitt for geometry." Mom laughed. "Mr. Devitt had a walrus mustache and . . . "

I didn't want to know about Mom and a teacher. I wanted to know about Mom and Adam's father. What if Mom dated him? I interrupted Mom and asked, "Did you ever go out on a date with Dr. Quigley?"

A tiny smile played around Mom's lips, and she sort of nodded. "Dr. Quigley took me to the sophomore homecoming dance."

15

"He did? You danced with him?" I couldn't imagine Mom dancing with anybody but my dad. "Where was Daddy?"

"I didn't meet your father until I went away to college. I told you the story. I bumped into your dad at the library and sent his books flying."

I was glad Mom was talking about Dad, but I had to know if she was really going to have coffee with Adam's father, so I asked her. I kept my fingers crossed that she'd say no, but she said yes. "Dr. Quigley is an old friend, Sara," Mom said, as if that explained everything.

Well, Adam's no friend, I wanted to say. And I knew for sure he'd start making jokes as soon as he found out his dad was going out with my mom. "What about Adam?" I croaked. What about me? What about Dad?

Mom reached over and patted my hand. "It's just a cup of coffee, Sara. Don't worry about Adam. I'm sure he won't bother you about it."

I started to say, "Are you serious?" But I didn't, because I knew if I did say it, Mom would think I was being a smart mouth and we'd probably get into a fight, and then Mom would get that sad look on her face again. So I kept my mouth shut. Mom

16

asked me about school and Mrs. Pitney. I didn't say much. The awful thought that Mom was going out on a date with Adam Quigley's father kept buzzing around in my head. Just wait until Jon hears about it.

Hey, that's it, I said to myself. Jon won't want Mom going out on a date. Not in a million years. Not in a million trillion years. Jon'll tell Mom not to go. And Mom'll listen to him.

She always does.

CHAPTER THREE

JON DIDN'T come home for dinner. I'd forgotten he had to work at Meyer's. Jon's been working at the drugstore ever since the accident. Mom and I ate lasagna, the microwave kind, and watched a rerun of *The Wonder Years*. We didn't talk much. It was a long night.

Pitney the Pits had assigned a math review paper for homework. "Can you believe it?" I asked Mollie when I called her. "On the first day!"

Mollie told me Bradford doesn't give homework the first week. Not fair. Right now nothing seemed fair. Why wasn't Jon here? I had to tell him about Mom and Dr. Quigley.

After my shower, I asked Mom if Jon would be home soon. I hoped I sounded as if it really didn't matter. "It'll be after ten," Mom answered. I could tell by her smile that Mom thought I wanted to make up with Jon. I did. If we were still fighting, Jon and I couldn't save Mom from making the biggest mistake of her life.

"Ten o'clock? How come so late?" Before Mom could say anything, I answered my own question. "Jon's driving Beth home." Mom nodded. Beth works at Meyer's, too.

Super. Now Jon wouldn't be home until ten-thirty or eleven. Jon says he and Beth are just friends. Ha! The day I believe that, Adam Quigley and I will be friends. Jon picks Beth up for school. Takes her home. Talks to her on the phone. He even takes her to the show. I bet he kisses her a lot, too.

Mollie agrees with me and she ought to know. Mollie has four older brothers and she says no guy is just friends with someone who is fall-over-in-a-

19

faint gorgeous. Beth is so pretty she can wear her hair in a little boy cut and look like Princess Di. If I wore my hair that short, I'd look like a guy.

Every time Jon brings Beth over to the house, my brain and tongue freeze. I never know what to say to her. It doesn't matter anyway. Beth is always so busy chatting away with Mom, she never even notices I hardly ever talk to her.

At ten-fifteen, Mom opened my door and said, "Lights out." Lights out didn't mean I had to go to sleep. I was staying awake until Jon came home.

Patches and I sat at the end of my bed and looked out the window. The moon was big and bright. When I was a little kid, my dad used to read me a poem called "The Moon's the North Wind's Cookie."

"Remember moon cookies?" I whispered to Patches.

I couldn't believe I fell asleep before Jon came home. I woke up at the bottom of my bed all cold and shivery. Patches was asleep on my pillow. The clock blinked out 12:09. Jon had to be home. Tiptoeing down the hall to Jon's room, I felt like a burglar. I didn't want Mom to hear me.

Jon was in bed. "Jon," I whispered, "are you

asleep?" No answer. I hate walking around Jon's room in the dark. I'd rather walk across a balance beam blindfolded, with my hands tied behind my back. If I knocked over Jon's Lego tower, he'd have a major fit. His tower won first prize in the castle contest when Jon was in sixth grade. Jon's been building things ever since I can remember. He wants to be an architect, just like our dad.

Rats. I almost knocked over Jon's guitars. He keeps them right near his bed. I don't know why. He doesn't play them anymore.

"Wake up," I whispered to Jon. I poked his back. "Are you awake?"

"Unhuh," Jon answered.

"I have to talk to you. Are you listening?"

"Unhuh."

I told Jon all about Mom and Dr. Quigley. "We have to do something. Mom can't go out with Adam Quigley's father. It's too gross."

"I'll take care of it tomorrow," Jon mumbled.

Back in my bed, I snuggled down next to Patches. "Everything's going to be okay," I whispered to her.

The next morning I woke up early. I was singing The Restless Ones' new song, "Smile at Me," when

21

I walked into the kitchen. I stopped singing. My heart fluttered and fell into my shoes. For one small second, I thought Dad was sitting at the kitchen table laughing and joking with Mom. It was Jon.

"Sara? Are you all right?" Mom asked. She frowned. "You look pale."

"I'm okay," I managed to answer. I didn't want Mom to know I was a complete and total pea brain. How can you think your brother is your father? They don't even look alike, except for their hair. Jon has my dad's black curly hair. And he's tall just like my dad.

Mom got up, came over, and felt my forehead. "You're a little warm. Are you sure you feel all right?"

"Yeah. I'm hungry," I answered, wondering how I was going to eat anything. I fixed myself a bowl of Lucky Charms, hoping they would just slide into my stomach. As soon as Mom left the kitchen, I asked Jon if he had talked to her.

"About what?" Jon asked. He swigged down a giant glass of orange juice.

"Don't be funny, Jon. You know."

"No, I don't. What are you talking about?"

"Mom and Dr. Quigley. Mom's going out for

22

coffee with him. Last night you promised me you'd talk her out of going."

"I did?" Jon shrugged his shoulders. "Why did I do that?"

Great. Jon didn't remember talking to me. I told him again. I talked as fast as I could because I didn't want Mom to come back into the kitchen and hear me. When I finally got it all out, Jon frowned and asked, "Is this guy a slime?"

"No. I don't know. He's not a *slime* slime but he's Adam Quigley's father. And Adam is a jerk."

Jon laughed. "Mom's not going out with Adam Quigley. Cool it, Sara. I've got to go." Jon picked up his books and headed for the door.

"Jon, wait. Aren't you going to tell Mom not to go?"

"No. Going out for coffee is no big deal."

How can Jon think it's no big deal? Mom can't go out with Dr. Quigley. Dad wouldn't like it.

And if Jon won't do something about it, I will.

CHAPTER FOUR

"HEY, KOVAR, my dad says your teeth are so bad, he's going to pull them out." Adam sucked in his lips and gummed his mouth.

I knew it! I knew Adam would say something stupid the minute he saw me. It could have been worse than awful, though; he could have said something about Mom. "You lie, Quigley," I mouthed and started to copy the long division problems Mrs. Pitney was putting on the board. I figured that if

I ignored Adam, maybe he'd get the message and leave me alone.

Zing. Zing. Two rubber bands hit their mark, my arm. Adam grinned and flung a black spider with wiggly legs right at me. It landed on my lap. I froze. I was almost sure the spider was plastic. It was the *almost* that made my heart jump. Adam is so weird he might have a real spider for a pet. "Cut it out, Adam. I mean it." I threw the spider back at Adam and, of course, that was the moment Mrs. Pitney turned around.

"Sara." Mrs. Pitney said my name with a frown in her voice. "Have you finished your math paper?" I shook my head. "Well," Mrs. Pitney said, and this time the frown was on her face, "I think you might want to get down to business. And I suggest you leave Adam alone."

Everybody turned around to look at me. I wanted to disappear. I heard somebody whisper, "Her neck is all red." I stared down at my math paper. How could Mrs. Pitney think I was fooling around with Adam? He's the joker. Not me.

Somehow I managed to survive the rest of the day and get home. When I opened the door after school, the phone was ringing. I answered it. "May

I speak to Mrs. Kovar, please?" a man's voice asked.

It was him. I knew it was Dr. Quigley. "Who's calling?" I barked into the phone.

"This is Mr. Clark from the Green Lawn Company." I never wanted to hug a salesperson before, but just for a second, I wanted to reach right through the phone and give Mr. Clark a big hug. Instead, I told him Mom couldn't come to the phone. I never tell anyone Mom isn't home.

Ten minutes later when Mollie came over and asked, "What's up?" I decided to tell her. I needed all the help I could get.

"You'll flip," I said to Mollie, "but we can't talk here." Even though Mom wasn't home, I wasn't going to take any chances on her walking into the kitchen while I was telling Mollie about Dr. Quigley.

Mollie stretched out on my bed. She thinks it's neat to have a bed near the window, and she loves my quilt. Three years ago when Mom, Dad, Jon, and I went to the Smokey Mountains on vacation, Mom and I found my quilt in an antique store. It's sky blue and white with red cross-stitching.

"Tell me what's going on," Mollie insisted. I sat cross-legged on my rag rug, cuddled Patches on my lap, and told her. Mollie jumped off the bed, plopped down beside me, and said, "You're kidding. You've got to be kidding."

I shook my head. "No, I'm not. It's true." Wham! An awful thought hit me like a wet snowball in the face. Adam's mother? Where was she? Even Adam Quigley had to have a mother.

"What's the matter?" Mollie asked. "You look weird."

I told Mollie what I was thinking. "Chill out, Sara," she said, "they're divorced."

"But what if they're not?"

Mollie sighed and rolled her eyes. "You watch too many soaps. But we'll find out—for sure."

"How?"

"I don't know. Let me think." Mollie scrunched up her face and chewed on her hair. She does that when she's thinking hard. "I know! I've got an idea. It's a good one," Mollie said, her voice rising in excitement. "We'll go over to Adam's house, say we're selling magazines, and ask for his mother. It's perfect."

"Are you wacked? I'm not going near Adam's house, ever. Come on, help me think of something we really can do."

Mollie frowned and chewed on one knuckle. "I've got it. We'll call up and ask for Mrs. Quigley."

"That's as bad as going over."

"No, it's not. Listen. Disguise your voice and ask for Mrs. Quigley; whoever answers will think you're selling something. People are always calling up and asking for my mom. Go for it."

"The Green Lawn man did call here today," I said to Mollie. "Maybe it'll work." I chewed on my lip. I had to know. "Okay. I'll do it. But we'll have to call before my mom gets home."

Mollie, Patches, and I raced back to the kitchen. I managed to dial, even though my hand was shaking. The phone rang six times before someone picked up the receiver. It wasn't Adam. It was a girl. It had to be Adam's sister, Laurel, Miss Stuck-Up Snooty. I covered the phone with my hand and said, "May I please speak to Mrs. David Quigley?"

Laurel said she wasn't there. I swallowed hard and asked, "When do you expect her?"

"Who is this?" Laurel asked suspiciously.

My mind went blank. Say something, I told

28

myself, before she hangs up. "I'm an old friend, from high school." Mollie clapped her hand over her mouth to stop from giggling. I gave her a shut-up look.

"What's your name?" Laurel demanded.

I froze. "She wants to know my name," I whispered to Mollie, covering the receiver with my hand.

"Make one up," Mollie said, still giggling.

I took a deep breath and said, "Mollie Smith."

For a minute, I was sure Laurel knew I was faking because she didn't say anything. I was ready to hang up, when she said slowly, "My mother lives in California." And then she hung up.

"I guess they're divorced," I said to Mollie. "But that doesn't mean my mom can go out with Adam's father."

Mollie and I went back up to my room with a plate of peanut butter cookies, two bananas, chips, grapes, and apple juice. Food helps you think. We finished everything before I figured out a plan. It was just like a spy movie. "I'll answer the phone every time it rings. And if Dr. Quigley calls, I'll tell him he has the wrong number."

"What if he calls when no one is here?" Mollie

asked. "There'll be a message on your answering machine."

"I always get home before Mom. I'll erase it."

That night the phone never rang. It couldn't. Jon talked to Beth for one hour, and then Mom talked to my aunt Monica who lives in Wisconsin for at least half an hour. And I talked to Mollie. Maybe if we keep the phone busy, Adam's father will give up. Maybe he'll never call Mom. And I won't have to lie.

The next morning, Mollie was waiting for me at the corner. "Did he call? Did he call?" she asked.

"No," I answered.

"Maybe he won't."

"I'm not counting on it. I'm answering the phone even if I have to jump out of the shower." I wasn't sure how I'd hear the phone in the shower. I guess I'll have to take baths.

For the rest of the week, every time the phone rang, I yelled, "I've got it!" Superman had nothing on me. I leaped over chairs, flew out of the bathroom, and raced up and down the stairs. Dr. Quigley never called. Maybe Mollie's right, I began to think, maybe he'll never call.

On Sunday, Jon took Mom and me for a ride in

his new car, the green bomber. We ended up at Brookfield Zoo. It was fun. We waved to the polar bears, held our noses in the monkey house, and walked through Tropic World. After the zoo, we drove to downtown Chicago. Mom treated us to hamburgers and Green Rivers at Ed Debevic's. The waitress snapped her gum at me and winked at Jon. Jon turned red.

When we got home, Jon announced, "Ice cream time." We had been too stuffed to have it at the restaurant. While Jon and I were making enormous sundaes, the phone rang. Jon grabbed it. "It's for you, Mom," he said.

"Oh, David," Mom said, smiling into the phone. "How are you?"

Slam dunk. My heart hit the floor. One phone call can turn the world upside down.

CHAPTER FIVE

"A BARBECUE? At Adam's house!" I shrieked. Mom had to be kidding. She knows Adam drives me crazy, bonkers, right up and over the wall. "Are you serious?"

"Yes," Mom answered. "Dr. Quigley invited us over next Sunday. It'll be fun, Sara."

Fun? I stared at Mom as if she had turned into an alien from another planet. How could Mom think going to Adam Quigley's house would be fun? Some fun. I'd rather be stuck in Mrs. Pitney's class for the next hundred years than go to Adam's house for even a minute. I looked over at Jon who was helping himself to more ice cream. Do something, I pleaded with my eyes.

Jon poured more syrup on his sundae and said to Mom, "It sounds great, but Beth and I are supposed to go to the Cubs game."

Whew! Maybe Jon was coming through after all. Go for it, Jon, tell Mom I can't go either. Take me to the game instead of Beth.

I held my breath and prayed, Please, please, please let Mom say we're not going. I felt like a sat-upon balloon when Mom said to Jon, "Maybe you and Beth could stop over after the game. Dr. Quigley wants to meet you."

Jon was my only chance. Say no, Jon. Say no!

He said yes.

How did it happen? "Why are we going to Adam's house? I thought you were just going to have coffee with Dr. Quigley." The question slipped out of my head and into my mouth before I could stop it.

Mom's eyebrows knitted together into a tiny frown. "I did," Mom said. "Dr. Quigley and I had lunch last Wednesday." Mom got up from the table and put her bowl into the sink.

"You did!" "Did you know?" I mouthed at Jon. Jon shrugged. He knew. Of course he knew. I was the only one who didn't know. I was odd man out in my own house.

"Mom!" Mom turned away from the sink and looked at me. "Why didn't you tell me? Why didn't you tell me you went out with Adam's father?"

Mom's eyes widened and her lips narrowed. I knew that look. I probably was going to be grounded for a month, but I didn't care. A kid has a right to know if their mother is going out with somebody besides their dad. Even if their dad is gone forever.

"Sara, I don't like your tone of voice." Mom sounded as if her patience had just snapped in half. Jon gave me a watch-it look.

Boy. Wait until Mollie hears this. Talk about feeling stupid. I had wasted a whole week racing for the phone. For what? Mom had already gone out with Adam's father. I wondered if Adam knew. Probably not, because if he did, he would have made a stupid joke.

Somehow I had to make Mom understand how

34

I felt. "Mom, Adam is . . . " I stopped. Mom was rubbing a spot right above her eyebrow with her fingers. If I didn't keep my mouth shut, Mom would probably have a headache, a bad one. "I'm sorry, Mom, it's . . . "

"It's all right, Sara." Mom sat down at the table and smiled at me. "I'm sorry I didn't tell you. But, as you guys say, it was 'no big deal.' I don't always tell you when I have lunch with Aunt Susan or Joanna."

Aunt Susan and Joanna are my mom's best friends. Mom smiled at me again. I felt like she was trying to convince me it was okay. It wasn't. "As I said before," Mom continued, "Dr. Quigley is an old friend." The way Mom said "old friend," you'd think she'd known Dr. Quigley forever.

"How come you didn't know Dr. Quigley last year when I told you about Adam? Remember I told you about the new weird kid that kept bugging me?" I couldn't help asking questions. They just kept popping out. I looked at Jon and Mom. I wanted to say, Why are we letting Adam Quigley and his father spoil everything, five minutes ago we were having fun.

"Cool it, Sara," Jon growled.

"I'll take care of this," Mom said to Jon. Then she said to me, "I just didn't make the connection, Sara. When we needed a new dentist, Mrs. Bascomb at the library recommended Dr. Quigley. It wasn't until I had my first appointment that I realized Dr. Quigley was the same David Quigley I knew in school." A little smile touched the corners of Mom's mouth. "I didn't know he was 'awful Adam's' father. Besides, maybe if you get to know Adam a little better, he won't seem so bad."

Oh yes, he will, I wanted to scream. But if I screamed at Mom I'd be in trouble up to my eyebrows. So I shrugged my shoulders and asked if I could be excused. Mom sighed and said yes.

Patches followed me upstairs. Sometimes I think she's the only one who knows how I feel. She curled up next to me on the bed and I whispered in her ear, "Mom and Jon kept a secret from me." Patches meowed, as if to say, "Bummer." I stroked her soft fur, watched the moon, and wished I was a little kid again, making moon cookies for Daddy. Daddy would understand. He wouldn't make me go to Adam Quigley's house.

The next morning Mom was waiting for me in the kitchen. She was still in her bathrobe. I wondered why. "Don't you feel good?" I asked Mom. What if I had made her sick?

"I'm fine, Sara," Mom replied. "Just moving a little slow. Want some toast?" I nodded and took a bite of Mom's rye toast. I had a feeling Mom was going to say something important. She did.

"I've been thinking, Sara," Mom said. "If going to Adam's house bothers you so much, I'll call Dr. Quigley back and tell him we can't come."

Whew! "Thanks Mom," I said. I jumped up and gave her a big hug.

When I came home from school, Jon's green bomber was in the driveway.

"How come you're home?" I asked him. "Don't you have to work at the drugstore?"

"I came home to see you. Mom told me you're not going to the barbecue." Jon glared at me. His eyes shot out sparks of anger. "Why are you giving Mom a hard time?"

"I'm not."

"Tell Mom you're going to go to that barbecue."

"No! Mom said I didn't have to go."

"Well, I say you do, or else."

I stuck out my tongue at Jon, and then I screamed as loud as I could, "You don't scare me!

If you don't leave me alone, I'm going to tell Mom!"

Jon blew out his breath so hard his hair moved. "Come on, Sara, Mom wants to go. Why is it such a big deal?"

"I don't like Adam. And what about Dad?"

"Dad? Dad would want Mom to have some fun." Jon came over and put his hand on my shoulder. "Give Mom a break. Beth and I are stopping over after the game. I'll keep Adam under control, so be a sport, tell Mom you'll go. It's a one-time deal." Jon squeezed my shoulder. "I think Dad would want you to go."

It was better when Jon was yelling at me. I could be mad. When he's nice, I have to listen to him. I sat down at the kitchen table and ran my finger along the edge. If I went, Adam would tell everybody in the whole school, maybe the world. He'd probably even tell Mrs. Pitney. It would be the most embarrassing day of my life. If I stayed home, Jon would think I was the world's biggest jerk and Mom might get a headache. What if she had to stay in bed all day? And what if Jon was right? What if Dad would really want me to go? I had no choice.

When Mom came home from the library, I said,

"Guess what. Adam acted almost human today."
It wasn't a total lie. Adam had been quiet. In fact, he'd hardly paid any attention to me.

Mom was quiet, too. She didn't say anything as she put the kettle on to make tea. I knew I had to tell her. "I'm sorry I acted like a brat. It's okay with me if we go Sunday."

"Has Adam changed that much? Are you sure?" Mom asked.

"I'm sure," I said and swallowed the lie.

CHAPTER SIX

"HEY, KOVAR, do you like French fried worms?"

Fun-ny! How gross could you get? Adam probably ate worms for breakfast and flies for dinner. But if I said anything to him, he'd say something embarrassing about Sunday. I pretended I didn't hear him and concentrated on dividing 76 into 1,502.

Pitt! Plop! A wet soggy spitball landed on my paper. Yuck! I flicked it off my desk and continued to work on my math. Maybe, if I was lucky, when Mrs. Pitney walked back into the room, she'd catch Adam and send him to Mr. Carver's office.

Zing! A rubber band stung my arm. "Hey, Kovar. Do you like your rattlesnake steak well done or medium rare? My dad is cooking them just for you on Sunday." Why couldn't Sunday just disappear from the calendar? If I were a magician, I'd zap it into the next century.

Sunday didn't disappear, it came right after Saturday, same as always. Mollie called me early in the morning. "What did you decide to wear to Quigley's house?" she asked.

"Jeans. My mom said I could. And my new sweater."

"Cool. You'll look great."

I didn't feel great as we drove to Adam's house. "We're here? Already?" I asked when Mom stopped the car in front of a red-brick ranch house. Mom nodded. When Mom and I walked up Adam's driveway, Dr. Quigley was standing at the door saying, "Hello, hello." I wanted to say, "Good-bye, good-bye."

While I was standing there hoping Adam had decided to go to the mall or the movies, a big black dog streaked through the door. One minute I was on my feet holding a plate of brownies, and the next minute I was lying flat on the grass. The dog was licking my chin as if I were a giant ice cream cone.

As I shrieked *"Mo-om!"* Adam raced out of the house. "Down, Shadow, down," he commanded. Shadow flopped down beside me, gobbled up the brownies, and wagged his tail as if we were long-lost friends.

Mom, Adam, and Dr. Quigley came running over to me. I wanted to bawl like a baby, but no way was I going to cry in front of Adam Quigley. So when Mom and Dr. Quigley asked if I was okay, I said yes. The yes was a whopping lie, because I knew my face was as red as my sweater, my back hurt, and my heart was thumping so loud I was sure everybody could hear it.

Dr. Quigley helped me up; Mom looked at me as if she wanted to say, "I'm sorry we're here." Adam did say "sorry." Then he said, "Shadow won't hurt you. She just gets excited when we have company. She likes you."

Don't like me, I thought, moving closer to Mom. It figured that Adam would have a monster dog.

Dr. Quigley put his arm across my shoulders and said, "Let's go into the house." I took a deep breath. I couldn't believe my feet were actually taking me into Adam Quigley's house.

In the kitchen, Mom whispered to me, "Are you sure you're all right?"

All right? Mom was living on another planet. I felt awful. I wanted to go home. But Mom already knew that. I was stuck in Adam Quigley's house. I gave my shoulders a little shrug and said, "Yeah." Mom gave me an I'm-really-sorry look and whispered, "We'll leave early."

Now wouldn't be early enough, I thought, as Shadow came up to me and licked my fingers. I moved closer to Mom. "Want to pet her?" Adam asked. I shook my head. "She won't hurt you," Adam insisted.

Dr. Quigley said, "Adam's right, Sara. Shadow's just an overgrown puppy."

Now what was I supposed to do? If I didn't pet Adam's monster dog, I'd look like a big baby and Adam would tell the whole school. I took a deep breath and rubbed Shadow's back. Her coat was hard, not soft like Patches' fur.

"Do you want to go outside?" Adam asked

almost politely. "Shadow'll fetch a stick, if you throw it for her." Some choice. I could stay in the kitchen and listen to Mom and Dr. Quigley chat, or I could go out with Adam and his monster dog. I decided to stay with Mom. I didn't want her to be alone with Dr. Quigley, but Mom's eyes said, Outside. So I went out with Adam.

If somebody had told me I'd have fun throwing sticks to Shadow, I'd have told them they needed a brain transplant. But it was fun. In fact, Adam and I cracked up when Shadow started running around the yard carrying a huge tree branch in her mouth. Adam chased her, yelling, "Superdog!"

We sat on the back steps for a while. Shadow plopped down at our feet. It was very weird when Adam and I started talking. He seemed almost human. I asked him how long he had had Shadow. "A year," Adam answered. Then he asked me, "Do you have a dog?"

I had just started to tell Adam about Patches, when Mom and Dr. Quigley opened the back door. "I hope you like barbecued chicken and corn on the cob, Sara," Dr. Quigley said. I wanted to say I liked chicken and corn a lot better than worms and rattlesnake steak, but I didn't.

44

Adam and I stood around watching his father light the coals. Nobody said anything. Then Dr. Quigley said to Adam, "Why don't you show Sara your baseball card collection?"

"Do you want to see it?" Adam asked. I could tell by the look on his face that he felt really stupid. Baseball cards are boring, but I knew Mom would give me the eyebrow if I wasn't polite, so I said, "Okay."

While we were walking back to the house, I tried to figure out why Adam was being so nice. Where was Adam the Dork? I kept my guard up, though, because he'd probably zing me with a rubber band, jab me in the arm, or say something gross any minute.

When Adam and I walked into the family room, Laurel, Adam's sister, was sitting on the sofa reading *Seventeen* magazine. She looked like she had just stepped off the cover. She was wearing a long brown skirt, a lacy blouse, and dark brown boots. "So you're Sara," Laurel said, giving me the once-over. "Adam is always talking about you."

"Shut up, Laurel," Adam said. His ears turned dark red.

Laurel stood up and said to me, "I'll show you my room. My mother helped me decorate it."

"Yeah, by mail," Adam said. "Come on, Shadow, you need a dog biscuit." As Adam walked out of the room, he turned his head and said, "Watch her, Kovar. She bites."

Laurel flicked back her hair, laughed, and said, "Adam belongs in a cage." For one tiny minute, I almost felt sorry for Adam.

"It's beautiful!" I said when Laurel opened her bedroom door. I felt like I had walked into Princess Di's bedroom. Everything matched, even the ribbons hanging from the canopy over her bed.

"Don't you just love periwinkle blue? It's my mother's favorite color. And mine, too."

I thought blue was blue, but I nodded and said, "It's pretty."

Laurel walked over to her dresser. "What do you think?" she asked, putting on a pair of silver hoop earrings that almost touched her shoulders. "My mother sent me these from Rome."

"I thought she lived in California," I blurted out.

"She does. How do you know?" Laurel frowned.

Why did I open my big mouth? I was beginning

to feel very squirmy. I shrugged and said, "I don't know. Maybe my mom told me."

Laurel smiled at me. It was the kind of smile you don't trust. "My mother is a flight attendant. She travels all over the world."

"Oh," I said. I knew it sounded stupid, but I didn't know what else to say.

"Sit down, Sara," Laurel commanded. "We have to talk."

I sat on the edge of one of the wicker chairs and wished Mom, somebody, anybody, would call me for dinner. "Did you say your mother told you my mother lives in California?" Laurel asked. Oh, no! I thought. I'm sitting on the hot seat. Laurel knows I lied. She knows I called, pretending to be her mother's friend.

A knock on the door can save your life.

CHAPTER SEVEN

"HEY, KOVAR, your brother is here!" Adam hollered.

Before Laurel could say anything, I jumped up and opened the door. As I headed out of the room, Laurel called after me, "Hey, Sara, I'm not through talking to you."

Want to bet, I thought. Jon was in the kitchen telling Mom and Dr. Quigley that Beth was sorry she couldn't come for dinner, but she had to go home. I wished I could go home. It was bad enough being here with Adam and worrying about Mom, but now I had Laurel on my case.

At dinner Dr. Quigley asked Jon where he was going to college. When Jon said he wanted to study architecture at the University of Illinois in Champaign, I almost choked on my corn. Jon was supposed to go to the U. of I. in Chicago. Why didn't he tell me? It's really hard to find out at a stranger's house that your brother wants to go away to school. How could Jon even think about going away? What about Mom and me? I put down my corn and tried to eat Mom's potato salad, but it wouldn't go down.

Between mouthfuls of potato salad, Jon started talking baseball. He gave a play-by-play description of the game. "Last time we went to a game," Adam said, punching his hand as if it were a baseball mitt, "the Cubs won. We're going to the last home game. So it'll be Cubs win, Expos lose."

Jon laughed. "I don't know, the Expos are tough. I wish we had tickets."

Laurel moved into the conversation quickly. She smiled at Dr. Quigley and said, "I forgot to tell you I wrote to Mom and told her about the game. Maybe she'll fly in for it."

The way Adam looked at Laurel I knew he was thinking, You've got to be kidding. Dr. Quigley frowned and said quietly, "You know she won't do that, Laurel."

Laurel smiled at Dr. Quigley and said, "Mom's a real Cubs fan. You never know."

Nobody said anything. It was as if everybody at the table took a deep breath. Boy, Laurel really says what's on her mind. I wish I could.

Dr. Quigley stood up. Maybe Laurel was going to get it. But Dr. Quigley didn't say anything to her. He asked us if we had room for Heavenly Hash ice cream. While Adam's father was scooping out the ice cream, Adam and Jon kept talking about the game.

"Hey, Dad," Adam said, "I've got an idea. Why don't we all go to the game? You said you can get extra tickets."

I could feel my mouth drop open. Adam, you nerd, shut up, I wanted to say. Laurel looked at Adam as if she really did want to put him in a cage. I held my breath as Dr. Quigley looked over at Mom. He had to say no.

Dr. Quigley raised his eyebrows, smiled at Mom,

and said, "Not a bad idea. I have a friend who can get the tickets. What do you say, Ellen?"

No! No! No! I looked over at Mom, pleading for my life. Laurel didn't know it, but she came to my rescue. "The game's a month away, Dad," she said. "The Kovars probably have plans." The way Laurel said it, I knew for sure she didn't want us to go. Well, I didn't want to go, either.

Mom smiled and said, "We'll take a rain check, David."

Whew! Mom got my message. A tiny smile played around Laurel's lips. Just as I was feeling safe, Jon threw a curve ball. "Could you really get tickets for the last home game?" he asked Dr. Quigley.

Dr. Quigley grinned and nodded. "Come on, Ellen," he said to Mom. "Cash in your rain check. We'd really like all of you to come. And if I remember correctly, you're a die-hard Cubs fan."

Adam's father needed glasses—couldn't he see that Laurel and I didn't want to go? I hoped Mom could tell we didn't want to go. Just say no, Mom, just say no, I thought, as Mom looked over at me. Mom hesitated and looked over at Jon. She didn't look at Laurel.

I looked at Jon, too. He had to be on my side. He'd said this was a one-time deal. Jon grinned at Mom and said, "It sounds good to me. Let's go."

Jon! You jerk! You traitor! How could you do this?

"Come on, Mrs. Kovar, say yes." Adam grinned at Mom. "We might catch a ball. I always bring my mitt." Adam punched his hand again. "It'll be fun."

"It does sound like fun, doesn't it, Sara?" Mom asked. Everybody at the table stared at me. It sounded awful. Terrible. But Mom doesn't really care what I think. She wants me to say yes. And so does Jon. Well, I'll just fool them. I'll say no.

Before I could open my mouth, Adam jumped up and pretended to throw a ball at me. "We'll have a blast. Bring your mitt, Kovar."

Mom, Jon, and Dr. Quigley laughed. Laurel looked like she was going to barf. What do I do? If I say no, Laurel will be happy. But Adam will kill me in school. And Mom will hate me. And so will Jon. They want to go. I don't have a choice. I have to go with them whether I want to or not. It's like being on a roller coaster when they put down the bar. You can't jump off.

I shrugged and said it sounded okay. Laurel glared at me. Mom smiled and so did Jon. Couldn't they tell I was lying? Couldn't they tell I was mad at them?

"Good job!" Adam shouted.

"Sara and I haven't been to a game for a while," Mom said, smiling at Dr. Quigley. "It'll be fun."

Fun? I stared at my plate. How could Mom think it would be fun? I guess because she wants it to be.

Adam and Jon started arguing about Ryne Sandberg's batting average. Mom and Dr. Quigley discussed the arrangements for the game. I looked over at Laurel. She looked as unhappy as I felt. She was biting on her lip and she kept turning her ring round and round her finger. I wondered what she was thinking.

"May I be excused?" Laurel asked Dr. Quigley. The way his eyebrows flew up, I thought he was going to say no, but he said yes. Laurel stopped behind my chair. "I have Michael Bolton's new album. Want to hear it?" she asked.

Before I could say anything, Mom smiled at Laurel and said, "We'll help clean up and then we have to leave, Laurel. It's getting late."

Laurel said quickly, "You don't have to clean up, Mrs. Kovar. Dad and I will do it later." Dr. Quigley agreed.

As we started out the door, Dr. Quigley said, "We'll walk you to your cars." We looked like a parade going down the driveway. Adam, Shadow, and Jon were in the lead. Mom and Dr. Quigley, chatting about the game, were next. Laurel and I were last. I wondered if she was going to say anything to me about her mother.

"We have to talk," Laurel whispered.

I gulped. Here it comes. "About what?" I whispered back.

"You know what. Your mom. And my dad," Laurel answered.

Hey, maybe Laurel didn't know I was the one who called. Maybe she knew how to stop her dad from asking Mom out.

"Meet me at the rock after school tomorrow," Laurel commanded.

I said okay.

CHAPTER EIGHT

"PATCHES? PATCHES, where are you?" She wasn't under my bed. She must be in Jon's room. Rats, I thought. I couldn't go and get her. I wasn't speaking to Jon.

I took off my sneakers and kicked them under the bed. I wished I could kick the whole day under the bed. Why does everything have to go wrong? Even my hair started giving me a hard time. I couldn't get my brush through the knot. It made me so mad I banged the brush down on the dresser. I didn't mean to shake Daddy's picture. "It was a terrible, horrible, awful day!" I yelled at his picture. Talking to a picture is talking to yourself, so I shut up.

I threw my clothes on the floor and muttered every bad word I knew. My clothes stared up at me. I hate messes, so I put them into the hamper in my closet and dug my sneakers out from under my bed. Then I flopped down on my bed. I knew Mom would be coming in soon.

Every Sunday night for the past year, Mom and I have been reading to each other. One week Mom reads a chapter of a book and the next week I do. So far we've read *A Wrinkle in Time, Freaky Friday*, and *Bridge to Teribithia*. We're reading *Homecoming* now. We didn't read last week, though, because of the barbecue fight. I was pretty sure Mom would want to read tonight. I didn't.

Five minutes later, Mom came into my room. "My turn to read," she said, smiling.

I yawned and said, "I'm too sleepy, Mom, I'll fall asleep." I could tell by the look on her face she didn't believe me.

"You were quiet on the way home, Sara," Mom

said. I shrugged. Mom continued, "I thought it went well at the Quigleys." Mom's eyebrows curled into a little frown. "I even thought you might be having fun."

Fun. Fun. Fun. I was sick of the word fun. I had an awful, terrible, horrible time. And nobody cared. I didn't want to see the Quigleys ever again. And I especially didn't want to go to a Cubs game with them. But Mom would have a cow. She wanted to go. And she liked Dr. Quigley, so I didn't say anything.

"Sara," Mom said, as if she could read my mind, "we don't have to go to the game."

Oh, sure. And, I don't have to go to school. And I don't have to brush my teeth or be polite to Dr. Quigley. "It's just a game," I said. There was nothing else to say. I knew I had to go.

"You're right." Mom leaned over and kissed me on the forehead. I wanted to grab her around the neck, snuggle my face into her hair, and hold on tight. Instead, I gave her a bird peck on the cheek.

When you can't sleep, you hear everything. I heard another cat calling Patches, I heard five cars drive down the street, and I heard Jon rapping on my door. "Sara, are you awake?"

I didn't answer. Traitor. Traitor. You didn't even tell me you wanted to go away to school. And you sold me out for a baseball game. I'm never, ever speaking to you again. I wished Jon could hear my thoughts.

Jon opened the door. I closed my eyes and pretended to be asleep. "Sara," Jon whispered. I didn't move. After a while, Jon went away.

A few minutes later, Patches scratched on my door. "Where have you been?" I asked her. Patches rubbed her face against my shoulder and gave a low purr. "It doesn't matter," I said. "You're here now."

Patches and I sat at the end of the bed. The moon made a path of light across my quilt. "How come everything is so mixed up?" I whispered to Patches.

Patches is a talking cat. She meowed as if to say, "What do you mean?" I told her what happened at Adam's. Some people think it's weird to talk to a cat, but Patches really listens. I told her all the thoughts that were buzzing around my brain like hungry mosquitoes. "Adam's going to say something embarrassing tomorrow. I know it. He'll probably tell everyone about the game." If you could run away to the moon, I would have been there in a minute.

Patches snuggled in closer to me and licked my arm. "It's all Mom and Jon's fault," I said to her. "I'm really mad at them. And Daddy, too." I didn't know I was mad at Daddy until the words came out of my mouth. More angry words came tumbling out as I buried my face in Patches' fur. "Dads aren't supposed to go away for a weekend and never come back." And then, as if Daddy was listening, I whispered, "If you had listened to Mom instead of going off with people you didn't even know, you'd be here. And none of this would be happening."

The whispers turned into a big hard lump I couldn't swallow. I hugged Patches hard. She jumped out of my arms and darted under my bed. I pushed my face into my pillow. It's hard to sleep on a soggy pillow, so I turned it over and curled up on my side.

I guess I must have slept, because I jumped when my alarm buzzed. Patches was sleeping on the windowsill. "Some friend you are," I growled.

I was still mad at everybody. While I was brushing my hair into a ponytail, I glanced at Daddy's picture. It made me feel all squirmy inside to be mad at him. But I was. I wondered if Mom was mad at Daddy, too. Maybe that's why she was going out with Dr. Quigley.

The house was quiet as I tiptoed down the stairs to get my breakfast. There was a note from Mom on the refrigerator. It said:

> Hi guys,
> I have a breakfast meeting at the library. There are bagels and oatbran muffins in the freezer. Eat something. See you after school.
>
> Love,
> Mom

While I was toasting my bagel, Jon walked into the kitchen. I ignored him and poured myself a glass of orange juice. Jon started rummaging around in the refrigerator. "Want some pizza?" he asked, as if he didn't know I was mad at him.

I buttered my bagel and said, "I'm not speaking to you." I left the kitchen and ate my bagel in the family room.

Before he left for school, Jon came into the family room, tugged on my ponytail, and said,

"How's it going?" When I didn't answer, Jon kept right on talking to me as if yesterday never happened. "I'm not working tonight, so I'll see you after school," he said.

Not if I see you first, I thought. Jon has some nerve. He thinks I'll make up, just like that. Ha! If he can find a way to get us out of going to the game, I'll think about talking to him, otherwise I won't.

"Come on, Sara," Jon persisted. "Lighten up. A Cubs game isn't a life sentence. It's just a game."

Just a game? That's what I said to Mom. Mom and Jon were talking about me. I knew it. Well, who cares? I'm not talking to them.

CHAPTER NINE

THE MINUTE we sat down, Mrs. Pitney started a time test. "On your mark. Get set. Go. Check your problems as you do them."

I usually hate time tests, but I didn't mind this one because Adam was so busy dividing and multiplying, he didn't have time to bug me. I worked the first problem. Great, I had the wrong answer. I chewed on my pencil, erased, and started over again. At the rate I was going, two thousand years wouldn't be enough time.

"Psst." I ignored Adam. *"Pssst."*

"What do you want?" I mouthed. I didn't want Mrs. Pitney to hear me.

Adam grinned and passed me a piece of watermelon double-bubble gum. "Gum helps you think. It's a scientific fact," he whispered out of the corner of his mouth.

Nobody had to tell me that taking gum from Adam Quigley was living dangerously. But if I was to finish my test, I needed all the help I could get. And who knows, maybe Adam's right. He's always getting A's on his math papers and he won third prize in the science fair last year. I popped the gum in my mouth and went back to working on my problems.

"Sara Kovar, are you chewing gum?" Mrs. Pitney's voice boomed out of nowhere.

Hearts can leap into your mouth. Mine did. I swallowed the gum in one gulp and shook my head.

Mrs. Pitney pressed her lips into a tight thin line. If her lips were a rubber band, they would have snapped. What if she told me to open my mouth? Old X-ray-eyes Pitney would see all the way down into my stomach. She'd see the gum sitting on top of the bagel I ate for breakfast.

What if Pitney called Mr. Carver, the principal, to come and look? Then another horrible thought started racing around my head: what if Mrs. Pitney called Mom? Mom would flip out.

Why did I take the gum from Adam? I had to be the dumbest person in the world. I wanted to yell, *Adam Quigley, this is all your fault,* but I couldn't. Adam didn't put the gum in my mouth. I did. Rats!

"Class, pencils up." Mrs. Pitney turned off the timer. "Sara," she said crossly, "I'm sure you know gum chewing is not allowed in my class." Everybody turned around and stared at me. I wanted to crawl under my paper. I gulped and nodded. Out of the corner of my eye, I saw Adam swallow his gum.

Mrs. Pitney addressed the class. "Class," she said sternly, "I hope no one would be foolish enough to swallow a piece of gum. It has absolutely no nutritional value."

I stared at my pencil and felt my cheeks catch on fire. "All right, class, resume test." When Mrs.

Pitney started writing on the board, Adam poked me and made an *O* with his fingers.

If Adam Quigley said or did one more thing to bug me. I'd, I'd . . . I'd *do* something!

At lunch, Mollie almost choked on her milk when I told her about Pitney. When she finished coughing, she said, "What a morning!"

"The afternoon isn't going to be any better. I have to meet Laurel." I groaned.

"Have you seen her?" Mollie asked. On the way to school, I had told Mollie all about the meeting with Laurel. I shook my head. "Maybe she's not in school," Mollie said. "Why don't you ask Adam?"

"Are you cracked? I don't want to ask Adam anything."

Mollie rolled her eyes. She pointed over her shoulder with her thumb. Adam was standing right behind us. I guess he didn't hear what I said because he held out his hand to me. "Want some gum?" he asked.

"Ha, ha!" I said to Adam.

The afternoon zipped by. How come time races when you want to slow it down? I chewed my thumbnail down as far as it would go. All I could think about was Laurel waiting for me at the rock.

65

What was I going to say if she asked me if I called her up? Mollie said, "Play dumb." How dumb could you get?

Mollie offered to go with me. I said, "Thanks, but I better go alone. I don't want an eighth grader to catch you at the rock." The rock is a large boulder that sits in a grove of maple trees near the school. It belongs to the eighth grade. No sixth grader ever goes near it.

As soon as the bell rang, I headed for the rock. Laurel was waiting for me. "Let's walk over to the creek," she said. I followed her. When we reached the creek, Laurel leaned against a maple tree. She didn't say anything. It was weird the way she kept staring at me. I felt as squirmy as I did in school. Finally, she opened her mouth and said, "We're not going to the baseball game."

"Great! How did you fix it so we don't have to go?"

Laurel brushed her hair off her face. "I didn't fix it. You're going to fix it so we don't have to go."

"Me? How?"

Laurel shrugged. "I don't know. Just do it."

"I can't. I triod."

"Do it," Laurel commanded. Her face looked as hard as the rock. "And tell your mother to leave my dad alone."

"Huh?" What was she talking about?

"Don't you understand? Your mom is hitting on my dad."

"She is not."

Laurel gave me a smirky smile. "My parents are going to get back together, soon. Tell your mother she doesn't stand a chance with my dad."

"It's not my *mom!* It's your *dad.* He's the one who started this whole thing."

"That's what you think. If you don't stop your mom," Laurel said in an ice-cold voice, "I will."

I ran all the way home. Jon had to be home. He had to listen. Mom was in trouble. Big trouble.

The green bomber was the only car in the driveway. Mom wasn't home yet. Good. There was time. I ran into the house. "Jon! Jon! Where are you?"

"I'm in the kitchen," Jon answered. "What's going on?"

"Mom! Mom!" I said trying to catch my breath.

"What's the matter with Mom?" Jon asked quickly, his face falling into a worried look.

I told him what had happened. Jon drummed his fingers on the table, then he shook his head. "It doesn't make sense."

"We have to do something. We can't go to that game. And Mom has to stop seeing Dr. Quigley."

"Dr. Quigley isn't that kind of guy," Jon said. "Why don't you call Adam and find out what he knows about this."

"Call Adam? Never!"

"What's this about Adam?" Mom asked as she came into the kitchen. I looked at Jon and Jon looked at me.

Chapter Ten

How do you say to your mother, "You're in trouble?" I opened my mouth to tell Mom what Laurel said, but nothing came out. Jon would have to tell Mom. Soon!

"What did you say, Sara?" Mom asked.

"Nothing."

Mom must have forgotten about Adam because she smiled at Jon and me and asked, "Guess what, guys?" Then Mom answered her own question:

"Mrs. Bascomb is retiring next month and . . . I'm going to be the new children's librarian."

"Way to go, Mom!" Jon said. I jumped up and hugged Mom.

"How about a celebration dinner?" Mom asked. Jon suggested spaghetti. I wasn't sure I could eat, but I couldn't disappoint Mom. As we were going out the door, Jon whispered to me, "We'll talk later. Okay?" I nodded. Jon must have figured out a way to save Mom.

While we were waiting for our spaghetti, Mom turned to me and asked if I wanted to go shopping on Saturday. "You can help me pick out a dress for my class reunion," she said. Mom asked Jon if he wanted to come with us. The way Jon rolled his eyes and said, "Thanks but no thanks," cracked me up.

It was fun chatting with Mom and Jon. It was almost like it used to be when Daddy was with us. Now we're a table for three. Jon, Mom, and I talked about Mom's class reunion, her new job, and we even talked about Thanksgiving.

Mom said, "I had a letter from Aunt Monica today." Aunt Monica is my mom's sister. She lives in Wisconsin with my uncle Kevin. Mom continued, "Good news. Aunt Monica and Uncle Kevin may be able to come for Thanksgiving dinner." That really was good news. Last year Thanksgiving was on the calendar, but not for us. Mom had a bad headache so she couldn't cook dinner. Jon ordered pizza. "This year, we'll have turkey," Mom said.

On our way home, while I was listening to my Walkman, Mom started talking to Jon. I took off my earphones to say something, and I heard Mom say, "Dr. Quigley called me at work today. He has the tickets for the game." All the good parts of the night disappeared like bubbles in a glass of soda pop.

After Mom closed her bedroom door, I snuck into Jon's room. He was stretched out on his bed listening to the last guitar tape he and Dad had made. Jon turned off the tape, sat up, and ran his fingers through his hair. I could tell he didn't want to talk about Mom. "You promised we'd talk," I said.

Jon raised his eyebrows. "I know. I still think you should call Adam and get the facts."

"Jo-on! I can't call Adam. Anyway, Laurel gave me the facts, so tell Mom."

"I don't know why you're so hung up about Adam." Jon shook his head. "Something is out of whack. And"—Jon rubbed his chin—"I don't know if it's a good idea to tell Mom."

I looked at Jon as if he had flipped out. "Why not?"

Jon hunched up his shoulders and sighed. "Look, Sara, Mom's not a zombie anymore. She even wrote to Aunt Monica. Remember how Mom used to spend most weekends in bed with a headache? Now she's laughing."

"Mom won't be laughing if we go to the game and Laurel says something awful." I took a deep breath. "We're not telling Mom to be mean. How can you just forget what Laurel said?"

"I'm not," Jon protested. "I'll tell you what, I'll find out what's going on. If Laurel's telling the truth, I'll tell Mom."

"How are you going to find out?"

"Trust me," Jon replied.

Every day for the next week, I asked Jon if he'd found out anything. And every day Jon said, "Hang in there. I'm working on it." How long was it going to take? Mom had to tell Dr. Quigley we weren't going to go to the game, soon, otherwise

Laurel would do something awful. If Jon didn't tell Mom, I'd have to tell her. That was a scary thought. What if Mom got those awful headaches again?

Why couldn't Dr. Quigley, Adam, and Laurel move to California? If they did, Mom, Jon, and I wouldn't have any problems.

I didn't see Laurel all week. Once I almost asked Adam if she was in school, but I caught myself just in time.

On Friday Mrs. Pitney was a giant crab. Her voice started to crack during math, and she had used up all the tissues in the tissue box by lunchtime. I wondered if teachers got embarrassed when they had to blow their noses every five minutes.

At two-thirty Mrs. Pitney declared a silent reading time. "I'll be right back," she said between sneezes. I figured she was going to the bathroom.

As I was taking out my book, Adam whispered to me, "Hey, Kovar."

"What?"

"At lunch my sister gave me a note. For you."

"For me?" I squeaked.

Adam nodded, grinned, and held up a piece of paper. It was crisscrossed with Scotch tape. "Give it to me."

"I have to read it first." Adam started peeling away the tape.

"No!" I reached across and grabbed the note out of Adam's hand. I was lucky Pitney wasn't in the room. She has a cow if you pass notes in class.

"Why is Laurel writing you a note?" Adam asked.

I covered the note with my hand and tried to act cool. It's hard to be cool, though, when the note you're holding is probably a bomb, set to go off. "I don't know," I answered.

Mrs. Pitney must have heard us whispering when she walked back into the room, because she croaked, "Isn't this silent reading time, Adam and Sara?" Half the class snickered.

When Adam started reading his book, I peeled the tape off Laurel's note and opened it. It said:

> This is a warning. Find a way of getting out of the Cubs game. If you don't tell your mother to leave my dad alone, I'm going to call her and tell her myoolf.
>
> Laurel

Oh, no you're not! The note sizzled in my hand. If anybody but Jon saw it, I'd die. But now, for sure, I wouldn't have to tell Mom about Laurel. When Jon saw the note, he'd tell Mom.

"What did Laurel say?" Adam asked.

"Nothing," I whispered.

"Let me see it."

"*No!*" I whispered, as loud as I could.

Adam leaned over and grabbed for the note. I nearly fell out of my desk but I held on to it. "Cut it out, Adam."

"Sara! Adam!" Mrs. Pitney croaked. "You know the rule about note passing." Adam and I froze in place as if we were playing statues. The room was so quiet I could hear myself swallow.

"Sara, please take the note and pin it on the board."

I stared at Mrs. Pitney as if she had commanded me to chop off my own head. I knew everybody was looking at me. "Mrs. Pitney, I can't. It's . . ."

"It's the rule, Sara. You know that." I stood there. My feet wouldn't move. Mrs. Pitney sighed. "Bring the note to me."

How could anyone be so mean? My hand started to sweat. I didn't know what to do. How could I

75

let the whole world read about Mom and Adam's father? I felt like I was wearing cement shoes as I started walking toward Mrs. Pitney.

Adam, like a big jerk, stuck his foot out in the aisle and I stumbled over it. Oh, no! The note fell out of my hand. Adam grabbed it. A weird noise came out of my mouth. Adam was going to pin the note on the board. Or read it out loud.

"Adam Quigley," Mrs. Pitney croaked, "what are you doing?"

Adam rolled up the note and stuffed it into his mouth. He turned Laurel's note into a spitball that saved my life. Just as I was thinking, Thank you, Adam, I realized now I couldn't show Jon the note. I was back at square one. And Laurel was breathing down my neck.

"Adam, put the note in the wastepaper basket," Mrs. Pitney commanded. I could tell she was really mad. Her cheek started twitching. She made Adam and me change seats with Todd Martinelli and Lisa Fitzpatrick. And then she said, "Adam and Sara, I want to see you right after class." I was sure we were going to be sent to Mr. Carver's office. Adam must have thought so, too, because he ran his finger across his neck.

Mrs. Pitney gave Adam and me an assignment. She told us to write a three-hundred-word paper on why note passing is not allowed in class. Whew! I stopped digging my nails into my hand. At least we didn't have to go to Carver's office. He might have called Mom.

Then Mrs. Pitney let us have it. "I also want you to write a letter to your parents telling them about your behavior in class today. Have the papers on my desk Monday morning, signed by your parents."

I shivered as if someone had dropped an ice cube down my back. Mom was going to ask me about Laurel's note. What was she going to say when I told her?

CHAPTER ELEVEN

JUST WHEN you think an awful, terrible day can't get any worse, it does. Jon wasn't home, so I couldn't tell him what happened. Mom wasn't home either, so I had to wait to tell her. I hate waiting. And when I walked into the kitchen, Patches ignored me. I had forgotten to fill her water bowl.

I was trying to coax Patches out from under the kitchen table when I heard somebody call, "Hey, Kovar!" It sounded like Adam. You're going bonkers, I told myself. No way would Adam come to my house. But just to make sure, I peeked out the window. It was Adam. Rats. He saw me and called out, "Hey, Kovar, open up! We've got to talk."

The last person I wanted to talk to was Adam, but I did owe him for the spitball, so I opened the door. Adam and Shadow walked into the kitchen. Shadow scooted under the kitchen table and tried to lick Patches. Patches had a fit. She hissed at Shadow and Shadow growled.

Great. Mom would have a giant cow if she came home to a cat-and-dog fight. Adam dragged Shadow out from under the table. Patches hissed at Shadow before she ran out of the room. "Is that your cat?" Adam asked. What a dumb question. Then Adam asked me another question. "What did Laurel write in that note?"

"Nothing." There was no way I could tell Adam what Laurel said.

"Nothing," Adam repeated. He scratched Shadow's head. "Come on, Kovar, give me a break. What did she say?"

I didn't answer Adam. I glanced up at the clock. Mom would be home soon. What if Adam was still here? What if Adam told Mom about Laurel's note?

"Tell me what was in the note," Adam persisted. "I have to tell my dad."

Tell Dr. Quigley. Oh no! I forgot that Adam had to have his paper signed, too. A big mess was turning into an even bigger mess. I couldn't tell Adam that his sister thinks my mom is chasing his father. It was just too awful to put into words. Finally I said to Adam, "Laurel doesn't want us to go to the Cubs game with you guys."

Adam rolled his eyes and shook his head. "Laurel's whacked. Did she tell you that my mom and dad are getting back together again?"

I nodded. I just couldn't lie. "Are you going to tell your dad?"

Adam made a fierce face. "I have to tell him. When my mom divorced my dad, she divorced Laurel and me, too. Laurel doesn't want to believe it; that's why she acts so weird." Adam shrugged his shoulders. "Come on, Shadow, we've got to go."

"Wait. Don't tell on Laurel." I was afraid if he did, Laurel would do something awful.

Adam looked at me as if I were way-out-wacko. "Don't you get weird, Kovar. Laurel got us in trouble. My dad has to know what she's doing." Adam opened the back door. "See ya Monday, Kovar. And don't forget, we're going to the game. My dad got the tickets."

"WHAT'S WRONG, Sara?" Mom asked when she walked into the kitchen. I was sitting at the table with my eyes closed, holding Patches and thinking about Dad. I wanted him to come in the back door whistling. I wanted this mess I was in to be a bad dream.

"Nothing," I said.

Mom frowned and put down the bag of groceries she was carrying. "*Nothing* sounds like *something* to me."

Mom is hard to fool. "I got in trouble in school."

"I guess you better tell me about it," Mom said. She sat down at the table, rested her chin on her hand, and waited.

Here goes, I thought. I took a deep breath and told Mom about the note, Adam, and Mrs. Pitney. "Adam made a spitball out of the note."

Mom's eyebrows nearly disappeared. "Who was it from?"

"Laurel," I answered. I stroked Patches' coat and I didn't look at Mom. I was waiting for the next question.

"Adam's sister?" Mom looked puzzled. "Why did she write you a note? What did she want?"

How could I tell Mom that Laurel thought she was chasing Dr. Quigley? The words just wouldn't come out of my mouth, but I had to say something. Finally, I told Mom the same thing I told Adam. "Laurel doesn't want us to go to the game with them."

Mom frowned. "Sara, I don't think I'm getting the whole story."

Sometimes I think Mom can look right into my head. I had no choice. I had to tell her something. Please don't let Mom get sick, I prayed. Then I said, "Laurel says Dr. Quigley and her mom are . . ." I stopped.

"Are what?" Mom drummed her fingers on the table.

"Are going to get married again." There, I said it. It came out. I don't know why I believed Laurel and not Adam. I just did. I snuck a look at Mom. She didn't look sick. She didn't look happy, either.

"I see," Mom said.

What did that mean? Mom gave me a tiny smile, then she got up from her chair and put her arm across my shoulders. It felt good. "It's not true, Sara," Mom said.

How did Mom know? "But . . ." I started to say.

Mom interrupted me. "Laurel wants to think her parents will get back together, but her mother lives in California and she's going to marry someone else, very soon."

"How do you know?"

"Dr. Quigley told me. It's sad, Sara."

Sad? It was crazy. Everything was crazy. Who was right and who was wrong? How could you tell? I didn't want to think about it. All I wanted to know was whether or not we were going to the game.

Mom sighed. "I'm going to talk to Dr. Quigley." Then Mom looked at me and said, "I don't think we'll go to the game, Sara."

"Okay," I said, but I thought, *Hurray!* Now maybe Laurel would leave me alone. Maybe Mom, Jon, and I could go to a game; that would be fun. I looked into the bag of groceries and asked if we could have the hot dogs for dinner. It was easier to talk about dinner. Mom said yes and suggested that I make a salad. Mom took off her glasses and said she was going upstairs. I hoped she wasn't getting a headache. If she was, Jon would kill me.

Jon walked into the kitchen while I was slicing tomatoes. He was whistling. "How's it going?" he asked. I shrugged. I wasn't ready to tell Jon what had happened. He might talk Mom into going to the game.

"Where's Mom?" Jon asked.

"Upstairs. Changing her clothes. Why?"

"I found out what you wanted to know. Laurel lied. Her mother isn't coming back to Maplebrook."

"How do you know?"

"Beth found out for me."

"You told Beth about Mom and me and Laurel?"

"Yeah. It's no big deal, Sara. Beth knows somebody who knows Adam's mother."

"Who?"

Jon frowned. "Why do you care who? The woman who cuts Beth's hair, that's who. She knows Laurel's mother. So Beth did me a favor and asked about her. She's never coming back. So quit worrying. She's getting married to someone else." Jon smiled at me. "We don't have to say anything to Mom."

"I already did. Mom is going to call Dr. Quigley and tell him we're not going to the game."

Jon hit his forehead with his hand. "You really messed up, Sara. I've got to stop Mom."

"No, you can't." Jon didn't listen to me. He walked out of the kitchen. I ran after him.

CHAPTER TWELVE

JON AND I fought in whispers. "Why don't you believe Mom and me?" Jon hissed. We were standing right outside Mom's bedroom. Even though the door was closed, we could hear her talking on the telephone. I was afraid she was talking to Dr. Quigley.

"Answer me," Jon demanded in a low growl. "Why do you believe Laurel?"

"Because," I answered, even though I knew it sounded stupid.

Jon raised his eyebrows and shook his head. "What's with you, Sara?"

"Nothing." I didn't know why I believed Laurel. I just did.

While Jon and I were glaring at each other, Mom opened the door. She looked surprised to see Jon and me standing there.

"Oh, Sara," she said, "I was just coming to get you." Mom's voice had a worry note in it. She hesitated, then she said, "I've been talking to Dr. Quigley."

I knew it. And I knew by the look on Mom's face we were going to the game. "Laurel is very sorry about what happened," Mom said. "She wants you . . . us to go to the game."

How could Mom believe that? She always knows when I'm not telling the truth. Why didn't she know Laurel was telling the lie of the century?

Jon gave my ponytail a tug and said, "I'm glad that's all straightened out." I knew the tug meant "keep your mouth shut." I didn't say anything.

Mom smiled at Jon and said to me, "Laurel wants to talk to you."

"Mo-om!" I just about shrieked. "I can't talk to her." I felt like I was standing in quicksand. The harder I struggled to get out of this mess, the deeper I sank into it.

"Laurel is sorry. She really is. I wish you would talk to her. But it's up to you."

Ha! Why do parents pretend you have a choice when you really don't? If I didn't talk to Laurel, Mom and Jon wouldn't talk to me. I'd be the black sheep of the family. "I guess I could say hi." Under my breath I muttered, "I bet a million dollars Dr. Quigley made Laurel say she was sorry."

Mom handed me the phone. My stomach started bumping its way down to my toes. "I'm sorry about the note," Laurel said in a robot voice. "I hope you can come to the game."

You lie, I wanted to say, but I couldn't because Mom was sitting next to me. If we had phonovision, I was sure I'd see Dr. Quigley sitting next to Laurel.

How come the harder you try not to think about something, that's all you can think about? The minute I woke up Saturday morning guess who popped into my head? Laurel! I blasted my radio and cleaned my room, but thoughts about her kept buzzing around my brain until Mom and I went shopping.

When Mom asked me what I wanted to buy, I decided to go for it and ask for wild strawberry lip gloss. Mollie will flip when I tell her I only had to ask for it once. Mollie's mom and my mom are always saying no to makeup. I wonder if Mom bought me the lip gloss because of the game. Mollie will probably say, "Who can figure parents out?"

After we bought my lip gloss, Mom and I hit every store in Oakwood Mall. Mom was looking for a dress for her class reunion. I liked the first dress Mom tried on, but she said it made her feel fat. Then I found a pretty blue dress, but Mom said it was too fussy. She didn't like the brown dress I found, either; she said it was too plain. I couldn't figure out why Mom was making such a big deal out of a dress for a reunion. She was just going to see a bunch of old people. After two hours of sitting on dressing room floors, my stomach started growling. Finally, even though Mom hadn't found a dress, she said we could eat.

On our way out of the store, Mom stopped at

the cosmetic counter. "What do you think of this color eye shadow, Sara?" Mom showed me a pale plum shade.

"It's pretty," I answered. Hey, I thought, good deal, maybe Mom is going to buy me real makeup. She didn't. She bought it for herself. Mom got into a long discussion with the girl behind the counter. Before they were finished talking, Mom had bought eye shadow, nail polish, blush, powder, two lipsticks, and a lip pencil. It's weird when your mother acts like somebody you don't know. Mom hardly ever wears makeup.

All through lunch I kept trying to figure out why Mom was acting so strange. While I was scooping up the last spoonful of my hot fudge sundae, a scary thought wandered into my head. Maybe Mom was acting like she was getting ready for a date because she was going to the class reunion with Dr. Quigley. That was it. I had to be the dumbest kid in the world not to have figured it out. Just to be sure, I asked Mom, "Are you going to the class reunion with Dr. Quigley?"

"I don't know," Mom replied. "Maybe. Would you be upset if I did?"

When I grow up, I'm never going to ask my

kids questions that I already know the answer to. How could Mom not know that if she went out on a real date with Dr. Quigley, Laurel would be on my case for sure? No way did I buy Laurel's I'm-sorry story. And Mom had to know Adam would say or do something that would be worse than embarrassing. He'd probably tell the whole school his father is going out with my mom.

And what about Daddy?

"Why are you going out with Dr. Quigley?" I blurted out. "Are you mad at Daddy? Don't you miss him?" I clapped my hand across my mouth. How could I have let those words out? I had to be the biggest jerk in the world.

Mom rubbed her forehead with her finger, sighed, and said, "Oh, Sara."

If it had started pouring rain right on us, right in the middle of the restaurant, I couldn't have felt more miserable. "I'm sorry, Mom," I said. "I didn't mean it."

Mom leaned across the table and put her hand on top of mine. "It's okay, Sara." Mom's lips smiled at me, but her eyes looked sad. "We'll talk about it when we get home."

I wondered what Mom was going to say, but

we never got to talk. When we got home, Beth and Jon were sitting in the kitchen playing Scrabble. They invited Mom and me to play. I really didn't want to, but I figured I'd better, otherwise Mom might think I was acting stuck-up around Beth. I surprised everybody, especially me, and won. Beth didn't believe that "yech" was a word until she looked it up in the dictionary.

Jon said, "Let me see."

I grabbed the dictionary from him and read, "Y-E-C-H, a gagging sound made in the throat to express disgust or contempt."

Jon and I yeched during the next game until Beth jumped up and put her hand across Jon's mouth. "You're next," she said to me. She laughed, and so did Jon and Mom. I didn't.

After three more games of Scrabble, Jon popped a giant bowl of popcorn and we watched old movies. I fell asleep while we were watching *Shane*.

Sunday night I was wide awake when Mom came into my room. I had waited until now to give her the paper I wrote for Mrs. Pitney. Mom had to sign it. While Mom was signing her name, she smiled and said, "We had fun last night, didn't we?"

"Yeah," I answered. I'd had fun with Jon and Mom. Beth was just there.

"But," Mom said, looking serious, "we missed our talk."

I didn't know what to say, so I didn't say anything, I just stroked Patches' coat. Mom walked over to my bookcase and pulled a book off the shelf. "Do you remember when we read this book, Sara?" Mom was holding *Bridge to Teribithia*.

I nodded. Mom sat down next to me on the bed. She held the book close to her chest. "We read this just about six months after . . . after your father died. Remember?"

I nodded again. I remembered Mom and I both sniffed a lot while we were reading it. It's a good book, but I didn't know what it had to do with Mom and me.

Mom kept on asking me questions. "Do you remember how Jess invited Maybelle to Teribithia?"

"Yes," I answered, wishing I knew what Mom was talking about.

Mom stroked the back of the book the way I was stroking Patches' fur. "It was hard for Jess to do that." Mom hesitated. It was as if she were looking for just the right words to say something. "We're a lot like Jess, Sara," Mom said quietly.

"We are? How?" In the book, Jess is a boy and he lives in the country. I didn't see how Mom and I could be like him since we're girls. And we live a lot closer to Chicago than the country.

"We lost someone we love." Mom's voice was so soft I almost couldn't hear her. "Just like Jess did." Mom was talking about Daddy. "But," Mom continued, "now it's time to invite people into our lives, just like Jess did, even when it's very hard. Do you understand what I'm trying to say, Sara?"

"I guess so." I knew Mom was talking about Beth, Adam, Laurel, and Dr. Quigley. But I didn't know why Mom wanted to invite them into our lives. We didn't need them. Mom kept looking at me. I could tell she wanted me to say something else, so I said, "I talked to Laurel."

Mom smiled at me. "I know it wasn't easy for you to do that; I was very proud of you. Your dad would have been proud, too."

When Mom said "your dad," a wave of missing Daddy washed up and over me. Mom must have felt it, too, because she said, "I miss him too, Sara." I snuggled in close to Mom.

After Mom kissed me good night, Patches and I watched the rain from my window. I whispered to Patches, "I can't tell Mom, but I'm praying it rains the day of the game." I prayed for rain every night for the next week.

On the morning of the game, I woke up early. When I looked out the window, the sky was a bright October blue. There wasn't a rain cloud anywhere.

CHAPTER THIRTEEN

"BUT WHY can't I ride with Jon and Beth?" Mom and I were in the kitchen putting away the dishes and waiting for the Quigleys to pick us up for the game.

Mom sighed. "I'd like you to go with me, Sara."

I didn't want to hurt Mom's feelings or risk a fight, so I stopped arguing. Five minutes later, Jon and Beth took off for the game in Jon's green bomber and Dr. Quigley pulled his car into our driveway. Mom sat in the front seat with him. I was the odd one out; I had to sit in the back with Laurel and Adam.

"Where's your sign?" Adam asked, holding up a piece of cardboard with *Hey Ryno* written on it in red marker.

"We don't make signs," I answered. It was a very long and boring ride to Wrigley Field. I don't know why Mom made me go with her; all she did was talk to Dr. Quigley about their class reunion. Adam read aloud every player's batting average and Laurel stared out the window. I kept waiting for her to say something nasty.

"Great seats," Jon said to Dr. Quigley when he and Beth found us. We were right behind third base. Adam whistled when the Cubs ran out on the field. "Go, Cubs, go!" he yelled, holding up his mitt. "Hit the ball here. Hit the ball here."

"Don't be such a nerd," Laurel said to Adam, giving him the stare.

"Takes one to know one, so just shut up, Laurel."

"Guys!" Dr. Quigley called in a warning voice to Adam and Laurel across Mom's head.

It was weird hearing Adam and Laurel fight.

They sounded like Jon and me. If they got into a really big fight, I wondered if we'd go home. Part of me hoped we would, the other part wanted to stay. I had forgotten how much fun a Cubs game could be.

Adam and Laurel stopped fighting when the game started. In the second inning, Ryne Sandberg hit a home run. Adam slapped me five. By the fourth inning the score was Cubs 2, Expos 2. My voice was almost hoarse from chanting "Go, Cubs, go!"

"Anybody hungry for hot dogs with the works?" Dr. Quigley asked when Montreal came up to bat.

"Me!" Adam answered, jumping up. "What about you, Kovar?"

"Okay." I was hungry. Everybody else, including Laurel, said okay to the works, too. Jon went down to help Adam and Dr. Quigley carry everything back.

While they were gone, Beth started chatting with Mom. I watched the ball girl give a new ball to the umpire and snuck looks at Laurel. "What are you looking at?" she asked.

My face caught on fire. Mom rescued me. She

turned to Laurel and me and said, smiling, "The Cubs are going to win today. I can feel it."

"Right," I said. "They always win when we're here."

Laurel didn't say anything. She just kept on spinning her Cubs hat around her finger.

"Look at him," Beth said. The Cubs had come up to bat and Ryne Sandberg was on the mound. "Isn't he the most gorgeous hunk on earth?" Beth giggled. "Don't tell Jon I said so." Mom laughed and so did I. Laurel acted as if she were sitting by herself.

Dr. Quigley, Adam, and Jon came back with our hot dogs just as the Cubs struck out. "Bummer," Adam groaned. He handed me my hot dog.

"Where are the napkins?" Laurel asked.

"I forgot them, so don't drip," Adam replied.

We ate our hot dogs and watched the game. Laurel poked me on the shoulder and said, "Your mother has mustard on her chin." Laurel sounded as if a mustard chin was the biggest joke in the world. Mom must have heard because her cheeks turned pink and she wiped her chin with a tissue.

"You're a real jerk," Adam said to Laurel. I

was trying to think of something cool to say back to her, when everybody jumped to their feet. The pitcher was hit with a line drive. "That really hurts," Adam said. "It happened to me once." Everybody cheered when the pitcher finally got up and walked off the field. We kept on cheering for the rest of the game.

"Cubs win! Cubs win!" we all screamed when a base hit in the ninth inning brought in the winning run. Adam jabbed my shoulder and chanted, "Way to go, Cubs! Way to go, Cubs!"

"We've got to celebrate that win," Dr. Quigley said. "How about a pizza at Leonardo's?"

The fun of being at the game fizzled away. I had thought we were going home. I held my breath, hoping Mom would say no to pizza. She said yes.

"Good deal," Adam said. "Hey, Dad, let's order deep-dish spinach pizza."

Spinach pizza? Gross. Adam Quigley has to be the only kid in the world, the universe, who likes spinach pizza.

"It's good," Adam said to me, just as if he'd read my mind. "We go there a lot. Laurel, Dad, and me. It's our favorite place for pizza."

I glanced over at Laurel. She looked like she

had been hit by a line drive. I knew she didn't want us to go to Leonardo's with them.

When we walked out to the street, the crowd pushed Mom, Adam, Beth, and Jon ahead of Laurel, Dr. Quigley, and me. We were caught by the stoplight. I stood right behind Dr. Quigley and Laurel, but I don't think they knew I was there. While we were waiting for the light to change, Laurel turned to Dr. Quigley and asked, "Do I have to go with you?"

"Yes, you do," Dr. Quigley said firmly.

"What if Mom calls?" Laurel persisted.

Dr. Quigley shook his head and jammed his hands into his jeans' pocket. "You've been leaving your mother messages for two weeks. She's probably in Rome or Hong Kong. If she calls, you can call her back."

I felt very strange standing right behind a private fight. And I felt a little sorry for Laurel. It would be awful to call Mom for two weeks and not have her answer. I was really glad when the light changed and we crossed the street. Mom was waiting for me.

The next week went by quickly. In fact, as weeks go, it wasn't too bad. I ran the mile and didn't fall on my face. Mrs. Pitney actually smiled at me when I pulled a B on my math test. Adam didn't bug me too much. I can live with a jab or two on my arm at lunch. I didn't see Laurel, which really made the week. On Friday, Jon surprised me. He came home with The Restless Ones' new tape, *Somebody Loves Me*. I almost flipped when he said it was mine. On Saturday, Mollie invited me to go to the movies with her and her family. She asked me to spend the night, too. Mom said yes. And best of all, Mom didn't mention Dr. Quigley, not once.

On Sunday, when I came home from Mollie's, Mom gave me the news. On Saturday night, she had gone out for dinner with Dr. Quigley, and they were going to the reunion together. I thought it was a dirty, rotten, sneaky trick for Mom to go out when I was at Mollie's.

"I can't believe Jon, he thinks it's just great," I told Mollie the next morning as we walked to school. "What am I going to do?"

"Make a Keep Out sign and put it on your front door."

"Come on, Mollie, stop fooling around. Help me. You wouldn't want your mother going out on a real date with Adam Quigley's father." Or anybody's father except yours, I thought, scraping my sneaker along the sidewalk as hard as I could. "What would you do?"

Mollie frowned. "I don't know. Pretend I was sick."

"It won't work. I already had the chicken pox."

"I've got it. Cramps. You could double over. They really hurt."

"I don't have my period yet."

Mollie rolled her eyes. "I forgot. Hey, I know what you can do. Pretend you have a cold."

"You can't fake a cold and I already thought about barfing. But I'd never be able to swallow anything disgusting or stick my finger down my throat. What am I going to do?"

Mollie gave me one of her looks. The look she gets when a wild idea is bubbling around in her head. "You could run away."

"Run away! Fun-ny. And end up with my picture on a milk carton after some weirdo captures me. Be serious."

Mollie shook her head. "I guess you'll have to do what my grandma says, grin and bear it."

"I'd rather barf." Somehow I had to figure out

103

something. I was so busy trying to figure out what to do, I almost didn't see Laurel Quigley standing in front of Mrs. Pitney's room. I decided to act as if she were invisible.

Laurel grabbed my arm as I walked past her. "Meet me at the rock after school," she whispered.

"No" popped right out of my mouth. I didn't even think about what to say.

"I have a plan that will stop the Brady Bunch routine our parents are doing," Laurel said.

Sometimes you just can't help yourself. I told Laurel I'd meet her.

CHAPTER FOURTEEN

WHEN I walked into Mrs. Pitney's room, she was writing on the board. All I could see were the words *Fun Fair*.

"What are you going to be for Halloween?" Lisa Fitzpatrick whispered at I took my seat. The class was buzzing about costumes. Mrs. Pitney tapped her pencil on her desk. We all knew that meant "shut up."

"The sixth grade is hosting this year's Halloween

Fun Fair," Mrs. Pitney announced. "That means we will be making Halloween decorations, drawing murals, and writing poems and stories." Mrs. Pitney paused; Adam was waving his hand. "Yes, Adam?" she asked.

"Are we going to do Ghost in the Graveyard?"

"*Booo!*" the guys howled.

"No," Mrs. Pitney answered sharply. "Settle down, class." She glared at Adam and continued to talk about the Fun Fair.

I was so busy thinking, You're weird, Adam, really weird, that I almost missed the rest of what Mrs. Pitney was saying. I heard her say, "I'll pass out the sign-up sheets now."

"For what?" I whispered to Lisa.

Lisa rolled her eyes. "For our parents. Sixth-grade parents run the booths and the haunted house at the Fun Fair."

"The haunted house?"

Lisa nodded. "When my brother was in sixth grade, my Mom was the greeting ghost."

All morning I kept telling myself Mom would never sign up for the haunted house. It would be too embarrassing if she did. I'd die if Mom wore a sheet and howled or said "boo" to people I know.

At lunch Mollie and I decided it would be okay if our mothers signed up for the fish pond or the win-a-bear booth. We were so busy chatting I didn't hear Adam sneak up on me. He dropped a banana peel onto my lap. "Thought you could use this with your monkey costume, Kovar."

"Ha. Ha. Very funny. Why don't you do us all a favor and go as the invisible man?"

Adam grinned. "Naw. I might be Frankenstein. Or maybe Dracula. Something cool." Adam turned to leave our table, then he came back and jabbed my arm. "Maybe your mom and my dad will work the haunted house together. That'd be really cool."

Cool? It would be awful. Worse than awful. How can Adam really like Mom and his dad being together? I bet he really bugs Laurel about it. I shoved my sandwich back into my lunch bag. Who can eat a peanut butter and jelly sandwich when their life is going down the tubes? Laurel was right, we have to do something quick.

"You're crazy!" Mollie cried, when I told her I was meeting Laurel at the rock.

"I have to go. You heard what Adam said; he thinks it's cool my mom and his dad are going out."

Mollie shrugged. "You better be careful or Adam's sister will get you in trouble. Real trouble."

"Thanks a big heap. I already know that." I knew for sure Jon would have a cow if he found out I was going to help Laurel. But I didn't have a choice, somebody had to get the Quigleys out of our life.

After school I raced to the rock. As soon as Laurel saw me coming, she started walking toward the creek. I followed her. "What's the plan?" I asked when I caught up with her. Laurel leaned against a tree and told me her plan.

"You want me to take the air out of the tires on my mom's car?" I croaked.

Laurel nodded. "I'm going to take the air out of my dad's tires. It's perfect. They can't go anywhere without a car. By the time they fix eight flat tires, the reunion will be over."

"How do you know how to take air out of tires?"

Laurel grinned. "I asked two guys in my class. They told me what to do."

"What if we get caught?" Just thinking about it made me shiver.

"If we get caught, it'll be worth it. My dad and

your mom will get the message, we don't want them going out. Are you with me or not?"

I shrugged. I didn't know what to do. It was like trying to decide if you should jump out of a falling plane or ride it out and go for a crash landing.

"Come on, Sara," Laurel insisted. "I know you don't want your mom going out with my dad. And I want my dad back . . . with *my* mom, not yours."

"I thought your mom was getting married," I blurted out.

"That's what my dad and Adam think. It's not true. My mother would tell me if she was getting married." Laurel stared at me. "So, are you with me or not?"

"I guess so," I mumbled. Laurel's plan was so crazy it might work. All the way home I thought about the plan. I wished I could talk to Daddy about it. He wouldn't want Mom going out with Dr. Quigley. Mom belonged with me, and with Jon. So I was almost positive Daddy would say, "Go for it."

That night at dinner, Jon said he and Beth wanted to take Adam, Laurel, and me bowling while Mom and Dr. Quigley went to the reunion.

"I know you'll have a good time, Sara," Mom

said. I almost choked on my stew. Mom's flipped out. And so has Jon. Laurel was right, if we didn't do something, we'd turn into a Brady Bunch rerun. Just thinking about it gave me a headache.

The morning of the reunion, Mom fluttered around the house. She made me vacuum and dust. While I was putting the vacuum away, the phone rang. "It's for you, Sara," Mom called out from the kitchen. It was Laurel.

"Do you remember how to take the air out?" Laurel whispered.

"Yes," I whispered back.

"Good. Do it at seven o'clock. Don't chicken out. I'll call you."

"Don't call—" I started to say, when I heard the click of the phone. Laurel was gone. If Laurel called, and Mom and Jon found out why she was calling. . . . My skin prickled.

Thinking about going out in the dark to steal the air from Mom's tires turned me into a total twitch. I yelled at Patches when she jumped up on my lap and tried to bat my nose. I spilled my glass of milk all over the kitchen table and let out a scream when Jon and Beth crept up behind me and said, "Booo!" Jon cracked up and so did Beth. I didn't think it was one bit funny.

By six-thirty, Mom was a total twitch, too. She must have asked me at least six times if I liked her dress. Purple is my favorite color, so I told her yes. Mom screamed, "*Ahhh*," and muttered under her breath when she smeared her nail polish. Ten minutes later, Mom couldn't find her earrings. I found them on the bathroom sink. All the time I was looking for the earrings, a little voice in the back of my head kept saying, "If you spoil the reunion for Mom, you're going to be sorry."

I went into my room and blasted my radio to the max. I didn't want to think about what I was going to do. I especially didn't want to think about what Mom was going to do when she found out she had four flat tires. What if she got one of those awful headaches? I prayed, Please God, don't let Mom get a headache. And I prayed God would understand and keep Mom from finding out I was going to let the air out of her tires.

At seven o'clock, I started out the door. The phone rang. I ran back and grabbed it. It was Laurel. "I did it. Did you?" she whispered.

"No."

"Do it, now!" Laurel commanded.

"What was that?" Jon asked as he walked into the kitchen.

"Wrong number," I squeaked.

Jon believed me. He started strumming on his guitar. Mom and Beth were upstairs. As I started out the front door again, Beth called, "Hey, Sara, come here. You've got to see your mom."

Mom was standing in front of the mirror when I walked into her room. She turned and looked at me. "Will I do?" she asked. "Beth did my makeup."

"You look pretty, Mom," I said. It was all wrong, though. I didn't want Mom to look pretty for Dr. Quigley. It was too weird.

"I'm almost ready," Mom said, fluffing her hair. "Are you ready, Sara?"

"Almost," I answered. "I have to brush my teeth and . . . and do a couple of other things."

I ran down the stairs. Jon was still in the kitchen jamming on his guitar. Patches was sitting in the hallway. She tried to sneak out with me when I opened the front door. "Oh, no, you don't," I said to Patches as I grabbed her. "You're a house cat. You can't go outside. The goblins will get you."

Patches dug her teeth into my hand. "Ouch. Stop that, you bad cat. You can't go outside." Patches jumped out of my arms and stalked off into the kitchen. She was really mad at me.

I closed the door quietly and walked outside. Mom's car was parked in the driveway right in front of Jon's car. Good.

I bent down and felt the front tire. It was hard and cold. I found the air nozzle. My hands started to sweat. I rubbed them on my jeans. I jumped up when the wind blew some leaves across the driveway. It's just a leaf, dummy. Do it. I knew Mom would be coming out any minute.

I leaned against Mom's car and took a deep breath. I could hear Jon playing "Take a Chance." Jon and my dad used to play it all the time. This was the first time Jon was playing it by himself.

The song made me lonesome for Daddy. So did the moon. It was just a sliver, hanging over the garage. If Daddy was with me, he'd say the North Wind took a big bite out of the moon. I knew what else Daddy would say: he'd say, "Sara, go back in the house."

I kicked Mom's front tire so hard I hurt my toe. Then I ran back into the house.

CHAPTER FIFTEEN

THE PHONE was ringing when I walked in the door. Mom answered it. Don't let it be Laurel, I prayed. If it was Laurel, I was dead in the water. "Hi, David," Mom said. Whew! It was Dr. Quigley. I never thought I'd be glad he was calling, but anybody was better than Laurel.

Mom was standing with her back to the kitchen door. I was lucky she couldn't see me. I know you're not supposed to listen to other people's conversations, but I couldn't help it. I had to hear what Mom was saying to Dr. Quigley.

"You have four flat tires!" Mom exclaimed. "Did you call the police?"

The police! "Uh." A noise gurgled in my throat. Laurel could go to jail. What if she told on me? I could go to jail! Don't be stupid, I told myself. You can't go to jail for almost doing something. My heart didn't believe me. It started to race as fast as it did the day I ran the mile. I thought for sure Mom heard the weird noise I made, but I guess she didn't, because she kept right on talking to Dr. Quigley.

"Oh, I see," Mom said.

What did that mean? Maybe Dr. Quigley wasn't going to call the police. Maybe he knew Laurel did it. If he did, Laurel was safe. Dr. Quigley would never send his own kid to jail.

I held my breath. If Laurel told on me, I didn't know what Mom would do or say. I should have listened to Mollie. Why did I listen to Laurel? I dug my nails into my hands, clenched my teeth, and waited.

"Don't worry," Mom said to Dr. Quigley. "I'll pick you up. The kids and I will be right over."

Great. I'm going to be creamed. It's not fair.

Don't make me go. Please. Please. I'd rather get stuck with a thousand needles than go over to Laurel's house. But who had a choice?

When Mom and I drove up to the Quigleys', Dr. Quigley was outside looking at his four flat tires. "An early Halloween trick, I guess," he said.

He didn't know. Dr. Quigley didn't know Laurel did it. I started breathing again. Maybe I was safe.

While Mom and Dr. Quigley were talking about the tires, Jon and Beth pulled up in the green bomber. "Oh, man," Jon said when he saw the tires. "They're really bad."

Dr. Quigley agreed. "I'll have it towed in the morning. I'm glad whoever did it didn't find your Mom's car."

Jon laughed. "That would have been a real bummer. But you and Mom could have taken the green bomber to the reunion."

Laurel and Adam came out of the house while Dr. Quigley, Mom, Beth, and Jon were joking and laughing. Even though it was dark, I knew Laurel was staring at me. All the way to the bowling alley, she kept on staring. It made me feel so creepy I started to itch.

The bowling alley was decorated for Halloween. Adam jabbed my arm and joked, "Did you get your monkey costume, Kovar?"

Before I could answer Adam, Laurel said to me, "Aren't you going to be a rat, Sara?" Laurel's words hit me like a punch in the stomach. I almost swallowed my gum.

"Shut up, Laurel," Adam growled. "Nobody's talking to you."

Laurel never said another word, not even when she threw two strikes in a row. When she walked over to the candy machine, Beth asked Adam if Laurel was okay.

Adam shrugged. "She's always weird."

Beth frowned and shook her head. "Maybe I should go talk to her."

Oh, no! Don't do that! If Laurel talks to Beth, she might say something about me. She might even tell everything. Then Beth will tell Jon what I almost did to Mom.

Adam saved me. "Forget it. Laurel won't talk to you," Adam said. "She won't talk to anybody. She's mad because our mom's getting married on Thanksgiving Day."

"Is your Mom really getting married?" I asked Adam.

"Yeah. Why?"

I shrugged. "Laurel said she wasn't."

"Well, she is." Adam cracked his knuckles. "My mom called two weeks ago and told her. My dad told her a couple of months ago, but she didn't believe him. She believed Mom."

Two weeks ago—that meant Laurel had lied. She knew her mother was getting married when she met me at the rock. Laurel was the rat. I picked up my ball. It was my turn to bowl. I tried to think about hitting the pins, but all I could think about was Laurel. Laurel the rat. She knew her mother was never coming back. She just didn't want Dr. Quigley to go out with Mom. How mean can you get? Mean enough to tell on me. I threw the ball.

"Gutter ball! Gutter ball!" Adam hollered.

Laurel walked past me, bent over, and whispered, "I'll get you, you rat."

That night, after I finally fell asleep, I had the most awful nightmare. I dreamed that three girls crept into my bedroom. All three of them looked like Laurel. They pointed their fingers at me and whispered, "We know what to do with rats."

"Go away. Leave me alone." I woke myself up shouting, "I'm not a rat!" I woke Mom up, too.

"Sara, what's wrong?" Mom asked when she came into my room.

"Nothing. I just had a bad dream."

Mom sat down on the side of my bed. "Do you want to tell me about it?" she asked.

What I really wanted to do was tell Mom I was sorry I almost spoiled her reunion. "I'm sorry, Mom," I said.

"Sorry about what?" Mom asked.

Everything. But if I told Mom about Laurel and the tires, Mom would think I was a rat. I shook my head. "I'm sorry . . . I'm sorry I woke you up," I said.

Mom gave a little sigh. "That's okay. Go back to sleep and dream sweet dreams."

"Did you have a good time at the reunion?" I asked Mom when she bent over to kiss me good night.

"Yes," Mom answered. Her voice had a smile in it. I knew she was glad I had asked.

After Mom left, I couldn't sleep. "Patches, where are you?" I called. I found her at the bottom of my bed under my quilt. She meowed when I picked her up. I put her down on my pillow and whispered in her ear, "Do you think I'm a rat?"

Patches stared at me. Her green eyes glowed. She stretched her back, put her paw on my shoulder, and kissed my nose. "I love you, too," I said, holding her close. Patches' kiss made me feel better. Nobody kisses a rat.

"LAUREL'S JUST waiting," I said to Mollie the afternoon before Halloween. Mollie and I were walking the long way home because we wanted to talk.

"Waiting for what?" Mollie asked.

"Halloween. Laurel's going to do or say something on Halloween. I just know it."

"Why Halloween? Is she going to turn you into a toad?" Mollie giggled.

"Very funny. I told you my mom and Dr. Quigley are going to run the haunted house at the Fun Fair."

"So?"

Sometimes Mollie just doesn't get it. "So I have to go to the Fun Fair with Adam and Laurel."

"So what? Your mom and Dr. Quigley are going to be there."

Mollie still didn't get it. "That's what's wrong. Laurel hates Mom and me. What if she says something about the tires to Mom?" Mollie shrugged. At least she didn't say, "I told you so." "It's going to be the worst Halloween of my life." Mollie didn't argue with me.

CHAPTER SIXTEEN

"MOLLIE, YOU can do it. You can *save me!*" I practically shouted the "save me" into the phone.

"From what? From who?" Mollie asked in a sleepy voice.

How could Mollie be sleepy on Halloween morning? For Pete's sake, it was nine o'clock. I had been awake since seven just dying to call her and tell her my idea. "From who? Wake up, Mollie. From Laurel."

"How am I going to save you from Laurel?" Mollie asked. I could hear her yawning.

"Laurel won't say anything or do anything if we stick together," I explained.

"How do you know? Laurel doesn't know me from beans and I'm shorter than you. I won't scare her."

"You're not that much shorter than I am," I argued. "And besides, being short has nothing to do with it. I know if we're together, Laurel will stay off my back. So, save me. Ask your mom. Please. Please. Please."

"Hold on, I'll ask," Mollie said.

I held my breath while Mollie put down the phone. "I owe you forever," I said to her when she told me her mom said yes. "Bring your costume over to my house. Dr. Quigley is supposed to pick us up at seven o'clock, so be here at six."

When Mollie walked into my room and saw my costume she said, "I like it. I like it. Next year, I'm going to be a cat."

"Where did you get the red mop-head?" I asked when Mollie showed me her Raggedy Ann costume.

"My mom dyed it. Pretty cool, huh? My mom

gave me her loafers, too," Mollie said, holding up her mother's black loafers.

While Mollie and I were getting dressed, an awful thought slithered into my head: What if Laurel thinks my cat costume is a rat costume? "Oh, no," I moaned.

"What's the matter?" Mollie asked.

"My costume! Laurel's going to take one look at me and say, 'Sara the Rat is here.' " Maybe she was right. Maybe I was a rat. Why did I ever even think about taking the air out of Mom's tires? I wished I could flip the calendar back and erase the day I met Laurel at the rock. Instead I plopped down on my bed so hard Patches yowled, jumped off my pillow, and flew out of the room. "How could I have been so dumb? What am I going to do?"

Mollie sat down next to me on the bed. She picked up my cat tail and waved it in my face. "It's a cat costume. Everybody knows that."

"Want to bet? Laurel won't. Help me. Think of something. We have ten minutes."

"I'm thinking. I'm thinking." Mollie chewed on her hair and stared at my costume. When she snapped her fingers and grinned, I knew she had an idea. "I've got it." Mollie covered her face with

124

my cat mask. "We'll switch. I'll be the cat and you be Raggedy Ann. We're the same size. It'll work."

"You're shorter than I am."

"Not much. You said so yourself. Come on. Switch. It'll be purrrr-fect."

I giggled. It just might work. Mollie's hair is as dark as mine. And her eyes are light green just like Patches'. Ten minutes later, Mollie was a cat and I was Raggedy Ann. I thought the mop-head might be itchy, but it wasn't. The only problem I had was wearing Mollie's mom's shoes. They were too big. "Stuff them with tissue," Mollie suggested.

"They still flap," I said after I stuffed them. "What if I fall on my face?"

"Chill out, Sara. You worry about everything."

When Mollie and I came downstairs, we fooled Mom for one half a second. "You two," she said, laughing, when she figured out I was Raggedy Ann and Mollie was the cat.

"You look spooky, Mrs. Kovar," Mollie said. Mom was dressed like a lady vampire. She was wearing a long black cape, fangs, and bright red lipstick.

While Mollie, Mom, and I were talking, somebody started pounding on the door. It was Dr.

Quigley and Adam. Dr. Quigley was wearing black pants and a black turtleneck. His face was hidden under an ugly rubber mask. "Good evening," Dr. Quigley said in a low spooky voice. "Are you ready to haunt a house?"

Mom laughed and said, "Yes, Lurch."

I didn't know who Lurch was, but he had to be a monster because Dr. Quigley sure looked like one.

"What are you, Adam?" Mollie asked. Adam was making a buzzing noise as he stood at the front door.

"The fly," Adam answered in a deep voice. "Buzz. Buzzzz."

I giggled and so did Mollie. Adam had covered his face with black glop. He was wearing black pants, a black sweat-shirt, humongous sunglasses, and wings. His wings stuck out of the black backpack he was wearing.

We were so busy asking Adam how he made his wings that I didn't even notice that Laurel wasn't with us until we were getting in the car. I nudged Mollie with my elbow and mouthed, "Ask Adam about Laurel."

"So where's your sister?" Mollie asked.

"She talked my dad into letting her go with her friends," Adam said.

I was safe, at least for a little while. When we walked into the school foyer, pumpkins, gourds, haystacks, skeletons, witches, and scarecrows were everywhere. Our class mural looked awesome. Adam and I hunted down our Halloween stories. Mrs. Pitney had said they were going to be hung on the bulletin board in the hall.

"Hey, Adam, look. Mrs. Pitney liked my story." Mrs. Pitney had written *Very good* in orange marker across the top of my paper.

"Guess what. She liked mine too." Adam grinned. "Maybe Mrs. Pitney turns into a human being on Halloween."

"Let's go. They have taffy apples," Mollie said. Mollie loves candy apples. We pigged out on cotton candy, too. I won a black derby hat playing Bozo's buckets and Adam won a cane. Mollie almost caught a goldfish at the pond, but it slipped away.

When we found the haunted house, Mom was standing at the door taking tickets. Mollie and I didn't say anything, but Adam said, "Hi, Mrs. Kovar."

Mom whispered, "Welcome," bared her fangs, and opened the door.

It was dark and cold inside. I knew it was my classroom, but I screamed when a monster pulled at my mop-head. Adam, Mollie, and I raced out the door when Dr. Quigley lurched after us. Mom called out, "Come back soon."

Mollie grabbed my arm. "Look. Over there." Laurel was standing across from the haunted house talking to some guys and two girls. The guys were probably the same ones who told her how to steal air out of tires. Laurel didn't see me. She was too busy talking and laughing.

"Let's get out of here," I whispered to Mollie. I wasn't taking any chances. So far Halloween had been fun, and I wanted it to stay that way.

For the rest of the night, Mollie, Adam, and I hung out with Lisa Fitzpatrick and Todd Martinelli. I didn't see Laurel again until she came running up to the car in the parking lot. Mollie, Adam, and I were talking to Mom and Dr. Quigley.

"Dad," Laurel said to Dr. Quigley, "can I drive home with Danielle and Robin? Please?"

Dr. Quigley frowned. "Mrs. Kovar has invited

us over for cupcakes and cocoa. I don't want you home alone on Halloween."

Oh, no! I almost croaked. If jaws could hit the ground, mine would have hit it with a loud thud. Mom didn't tell me the cupcakes she baked were for the Quigleys. Now Laurel would say something for sure. Mom and Dr. Quigley were doing the Brady Bunch routine again.

Laurel didn't say anything. Mom did. And I couldn't believe what she said. Mom said, "I know Danielle's mother and I'm sure she wouldn't mind driving Laurel to our house. It's not out of her way."

Laurel gave Mom a startled look. When Dr. Quigley agreed with Mom's suggestion, Laurel said, "Thanks," and took off.

I didn't say anything all the way home. I knew something awful was going to happen the minute Laurel walked through the door.

When Mom opened the front door, Patches would have darted outside if I hadn't grabbed her. "You can't go out, Patches," I scolded. Patches jumped out of my arms and flounced out of the room, her tail high in the air. She was mad at me again.

Ten minutes later, the doorbell rang. Laurel! It had to be Laurel. Who was going to open the door? Mollie was in the upstairs bathroom. Adam was in the downstairs bathroom. Mom, Dr. Quigley, and Patches were in the kitchen. No way was I going to open the door.

When the doorbell rang again, Mom called from the kitchen, "Sara, answer the door, please."

Great. Now what was I going to do? Why did Jon have to be out with Beth? The doorbell rang again.

"Sara!" Mom called. "Did you hear me?" I knew Mom meant "open the door, *now!*" I didn't have a choice.

Laurel laughed when she saw me. "You should wear a mop-head all the time."

Ha, ha. How come when somebody says something really mean to you, your brain shuts down?

CHAPTER SEVENTEEN

"WHAT'S WITH Laurel?" Mollie whispered to me.

I shrugged. Something was going on with Laurel, but I didn't know what. When she saw Mollie, she said, "Cool costume." Then she asked Adam where he won the cane and petted Patches until she purred. She was sticky sweet to everyone but me.

Now she was out in the kitchen with Mom and Dr. Quigley. Mollie, Adam, and I were in the family room, eating Mom's cupcakes and watching *Dark Shadows*.

"Ask Adam what's going on," Mollie mouthed.

We could hear Laurel, Mom, and Dr. Quigley laughing. The next thing I heard was Laurel telling Mom she just loved chocolate cupcakes with orange frosting. It was scary hearing Laurel being nice to Mom. What if she told Mom about the tires? What if she told Mom it was my idea? I wanted to jump up, run into the kitchen, and say, "She lies. Don't believe her, Mom. Don't believe anything she says." But I couldn't. Not with Dr. Quigley sitting there; he'd ask me questions. And so would Mom.

"Ask Adam what's going on," Mollie mouthed again.

"You ask him," I mouthed back.

"What are you guys talking about?" Adam asked.

"Your sister," Mollie answered.

"What about her?"

"How come she's being so nice to my mom?" The question popped out of my mouth before I knew I was going to ask it.

Adam shrugged. "Who knows? I think my dad said something to her."

"Time to go, guys," Dr. Quigley said, coming into the room. Mom and Laurel were right behind him. Dr. Quigley turned to Mom and said, "I'll call you tomorrow, Ellen. And thanks for the Thanksgiving dinner invitation." He smiled at Mom. "We'll be here."

Thanksgiving dinner! Mom! How could you ask them? Don't you know our house is the last place Laurel wants to be?

Laurel walked over to me and whispered, "Meet me at the rock, Monday." I turned into a giant goosebump.

While Mom and I were straightening up the kitchen, I took a deep breath and said, "Mom, I thought Aunt Monica and Uncle Kevin were coming for Thanksgiving."

"They *are* coming, Sara."

"But won't Aunt Monica and Uncle Kevin think it's weird, having Thanksgiving dinner with Dr. Quigley, Adam, and Laurel?"

"Why would they think it's weird?" Mom asked.

"I don't know. They don't know them."

"Sara." Mom shook her head. "Having the Quigleys for dinner will be just fine with Aunt Monica and Uncle Kevin."

Well, it's not fine with me, I wanted to say. Instead, I asked, "What about Laurel? She won't want to come." You dummy, I thought, why did you say that? Why did you bring up Laurel?

"Laurel?" Mom frowned. "She didn't seem to mind coming tonight."

My eyes almost rolled up into my head. How could Mom think that? Couldn't she see Laurel was faking it? My brain answered the question. Mom doesn't see because she wants everybody to like everybody. Fat chance. Laurel will never like us . . . especially me. And I'll never like her.

Mom put her arm across my shoulder and gave me a little hug. "It's going to be okay, Sara."

Okay? Sometimes parents don't know anything. How could it be okay? I knew for sure if I didn't stop Thanksgiving, Laurel was going to do something awful. I had to get Mom to change her mind. Take back the invitation. If I didn't . . . I shivered. It was too scary to think about.

But when I crawled into bed, that was all I could think about. "Patches, where are you?" I whispered. I needed to hold her tight. Patches wasn't in my room. She was probably asleep on the La-Z-Boy in the family room.

I crept down the stairs. I didn't want to wake up Mom. She might want to talk and I was all talked out.

Patches wasn't on the La-Z-Boy. I couldn't find her anywhere. "Patches, where are you?" I whispered as loud as I could.

"Right here," Jon said, walking into the family room. He was carrying Patches.

"Where was she?"

"On the front porch. How did she get out?"

"Probably with the Quigleys."

"Ooh. Aren't we a little hostile?" Jon flopped down on the couch. "Want to talk about it?"

I shrugged. Jon pulled a bag of peanut butter cups out of his pocket. "Beth sent these to you."

"She did?" I knew I sounded surprised. "Tell her I said thanks."

"You tell her. Beth says you hardly ever talk to her."

Great. Now Beth was mad at me. How could she think I don't talk to her? That's crazy. I felt like everybody, everything, the whole world, was mixed up, backward, upside down. "I'm going to bed," I said, picking up Patches. She jumped out of my arms. "Patches," I called after her. Patches didn't pay any attention to me. She headed for the kitchen. "So go away, you dumb cat. Be mad. See if I care."

"Hey," Jon said. He came after me and tugged on my ponytail. "We'll give Patches some tuna. That'll put her in a better mood. And for us, a double chocolate milk. What do you say?"

I said okay. While we were sipping our milk, I asked Jon if he knew about Thanksgiving. He said no.

"Do you want them to come?" I asked.

"Sure. If it makes Mom happy, why not?"

I didn't answer him.

Jon frowned. "What's going on, Sara?"

I shrugged, snapped my fingernails against the edge of the table, and muttered, "I don't want them to come."

"Why? They were here tonight."

"I know. But Thanksgiving is different."

Jon frowned. "I don't get it. What makes it different?"

"It just is." Jon never does anything really stupid, so how could I tell him about Laurel, and the tires, and the mess I was in? "You're lucky," I said.

"I am? Why?"

"You never do anything dumb."

Jon laughed. "Oh, sure. How about the time I took Vinnie Parker's dare and flushed a tennis ball down the toilet and nearly flooded the school?"

"That was funny."

"It was stupid."

"Why did you do it?"

"Because I was scared of Vinnie Parker. I was sure he'd beat me up if I didn't take the dare. And then he beat me up anyway. That's why Dad signed me up for karate lessons."

"I wish I knew karate."

Jon put down his glass of milk. "Why? Who are you afraid of?"

"Nobody."

"Come on, Sara. Who are you afraid of?"

Why did I open my big mouth? Now I have to tell Jon. He won't give up until I do. I sucked in my breath and said, "Laurel Quigley." I waited for him to laugh.

He didn't. "Laurel? Why are you scared of her?" he asked.

Before I could stop myself, I told him. Then, like a big baby, I started crying.

"Come on, Sara. You didn't take the air out of Mom's tires and that's what counts."

"What about Laurel? What if she tells Mom? What if she tells Mom it was my idea?" I asked between sniffles.

"You can do something about that."

"What? Punch her out?"

Jon laughed and shook his head. "Laurel can't blackmail you if Mom knows about the tires."

"How's Mom going to find out? Uhhh!" An awful thought hit me. "Are you going to tell Mom?"

Jon shook his head. "No! Hey, you know I wouldn't do that."

Since Jon wasn't going to tell Mom and I knew Mollie would never open her mouth, the only other person, besides Laurel, who might was me. "You think . . . you think I should tell Mom?"

Jon nodded.

How could I tell on myself?

CHAPTER EIGHTEEN

WHO CAN sleep when their brain is playing Ping-Pong? Tell Mom! Ping! No, I can't tell her. Pong! Ping-Pong. Ping-Pong. Finally I told myself to shut up, then I put my pillow over my ears and fell asleep.

When I woke up, I knew I couldn't tell Mom about the tires. She'd get a headache, probably the worst headache of her whole life, and it would be all my fault.

But what about Laurel? Tomorrow Laurel would be waiting for me at the rock. It was a rerun of a rerun. I had to do something.

I decided to clean my room. I dumped all my books in the middle of the floor, piled my stuffed animals on top of them, and pulled the sheets and quilt off the bed. What a mess. I sat down next to the pile, picked up my quilt, and rubbed the edge of it against my cheek. It's weird how one thing can make you think about something else. My quilt made me think about my dad. Daddy was with Mom and me when we found it in the antique store. He wasn't with us now. I folded up my quilt and put it back on the pile. My room could wait.

When I went downstairs, Jon was outside polishing the green bomber. Mom was in the kitchen practicing her speech for the library board brunch. She was the guest speaker. "Do you feel all right, Sara?" Mom asked when she saw me. Sometimes Mom has X-ray eyes, just like Mrs. Pitney.

"I'm okay," I answered, hoping Mom believed me. I opened a box of Cheerios, ate two, and then put the box back in the cabinet.

"You're not eating." Mom frowned. "Do you want an egg? I'll scramble one for you."

"An egg?" Yuck. I shook my head. Thinking about food made my stomach squirm.

Mom walked over to me and put her hand on my forehead. "You have circles under your eyes. Didn't you sleep?"

"I slept. I'm just not hungry." I was glad Mom was leaving. If she stayed home and kept on asking me questions, everything might spill out.

Patches was sleeping on the top of the couch when I walked into the family room. She jumped into my lap as I clicked on the TV. News. News. News. Boring. Boring. Boring. Math for Modern Living. No way. Wrestling. Ugh. I switched to the movie channel. Great, just great, I had seen them all. Next, I tried the rerun channel. "Oh no!" I snapped off a Brady Bunch rerun. "It's not fair," I said to Patches.

"What's not fair?" Mom asked, coming into the room.

"Sunday shows. They stink," I answered quickly. "There's nothing on. There's nothing to do."

"You could do your homework."

"I don't have any."

"Call Mollie."

141

"I can't. She's not home. She's at church." I folded my arms across my chest and stared at the blank TV sceen. "There's nothing to do. There's never anything to do around here." Mom sighed. I knew if I didn't stop acting like a brat, she was going to get mad. Maybe I wanted her to. Maybe it would be better if she got mad at me for something else besides the tires.

"Well, do something, Sara. Why don't you make brownies? There's a box of mix in the pantry." I shrugged. Mom's eyebrows shot up over her glasses. "I'm going upstairs. I want to finish my letter to Aunt Monica before I go."

"Are you going to tell Aunt Monica about the Quigleys?"

Mom stopped on the stairs. She turned around. "Is that what's wrong? Are you upset because the Quigleys are coming for Thanksgiving dinner?"

"No," I answered. It wasn't a total lie. I really didn't care if Adam and Dr. Quigley came for Thanksgiving. It was Laurel who couldn't come.

"Are you sure?" Mom asked. She came over and sat down next to me. "Sara, what's bothering you?"

I shrugged and told a giant lie. "Nothing's bothering me."

Mom rubbed her finger across her forehead. "I wish you'd talk to me, Sara. I thought you were beginning to like the Quigleys. You seemed to have a good time at the Fun Fair."

"I did." It was true. I didn't really mind being with Adam and Dr. Quigley. It was Laurel who was causing all the problems.

"Sara, does this have anything to do with Laurel?"

I didn't answer Mom. Two lies in a row are two too many lies.

Mom didn't give up. "Why didn't you want to let Laurel into the house last night?" she asked.

How did Mom know? "Because . . ." I gulped and kept my mouth shut.

"Because why, Sara?"

"Because of the tires." The words started tumbling out. They just wouldn't stay inside any longer. I told Mom everything. I told her about Laurel, the Brady Brunch routine, me and the tires. I even told her I prayed for rain the day of the Cubs game. Once the words were out, I wanted to grab them back. I bit down on my lip and stared at my hands. I couldn't look at Mom.

"Look at me, Sara," Mom said in a soft voice. "I'm glad you told me."

"You are? You're not mad?"

"No." Mom shook her head and smiled a little smile. "You didn't do anything, Sara."

"I almost did."

"*Almost* doesn't count."

If Mom wasn't mad, maybe *almost* didn't count as much as I thought it did. If I'd really taken the air out of Mom's tires, I knew I'd want to go and live in a rat hole. I gave a little shiver. "I'm sorry I even thought about it, Mom."

"Being sorry is what counts, Sara." Mom leaned over and kissed my cheek. "I'm glad we talked."

"Me, too," I whispered, and moved closer to Mom. Just as I was feeling better, an awful thought popped into my head. What if Mom tells Dr. Quigley about Laurel? If Laurel finds out I blabbed, even karate lessons wouldn't help. "Mom, are you . . . are you going to tell Dr. Quigley about Laurel and me?"

"No," Mom answered. "What Laurel did is between Dr. Quigley and Laurel." Mom smiled and brushed a wisp of hair off my face. "Sara, I'm sure

Laurel is just as sorry as you are. I know she talks to her dad just like you talk to me."

Did Mom mean Laurel told on herself, too? No way! But maybe Mom knew something I didn't know. What if Mom already knew about Laurel, me, and the tires? Maybe Mom was just waiting for me to tell her. I'm really glad I did.

After Mom left, I cleaned up my room. It didn't take me too long. I stuffed the sheets down the clothes chute, made my bed, fluffed the pillows, smoothed my quilt, dusted, rearranged my animals on the shelf, and put my books back in the bookcase. I didn't take the time to put them in any order. I wanted to surprise Mom with brownies when she came home from the brunch.

Jon came into the kitchen strumming his guitar while I was making chocolate frosting. "Did you tell Mom?" he asked.

I nodded.

"Good job. Mom didn't yell at you, did she?"

"No." I told Jon about talking to Mom while we licked the frosting off the beaters. "Do you think Laurel told on herself?" I asked him. Jon thought she did. "Do you think Dr. Quigley yelled at her?"

"Probably. Dad would have yelled at you if you let the air out of Mom's tires. But"—Jon smiled at me—"he wouldn't have stayed mad forever."

"I know that." I dug the spoon deep into the frosting bowl. "Jon, do you think Dad still knows what we do?"

At first, Jon didn't answer me. He picked up his guitar and started tuning it, then he said, "Yeah, I think so."

"Me, too." I frosted all the brownies, gave one to Jon, and said, "I heard you playing 'Take a Chance' the other night. It sounded good." Jon played it again.

That night, when I finally got to talk to Mollie, I told her everything that had happened. "Hey, that means you don't have to meet Laurel at the rock tomorrow," Mollie said.

The rock. I was feeling so good about telling Mom, I had forgotten all about meeting Laurel. Maybe Jon could give me a quick karate lesson.

Monday afternoon, right after school, I met Mollie on the school steps. "Do you want me to go with you?" she asked.

I did want Mollie to go with me, but I told her

I'd better go alone. Some things you just have to do by yourself.

"I'll be here when you get back," Mollie said. She sat down on the steps.

Adam wheeled up on his bike while Mollie and I were talking. "Where's your mop-head, Kovar?"

"Ha. Ha. Go spin in space, Adam."

Adam spun the pedals on his bike and laughed. "So, where are you going?"

"I have to meet someone." I had a feeling it wouldn't be a good idea to tell Adam I was meeting Laurel. I didn't want to start a family fight. "So, where are *you* going?" I asked him.

"Nowhere. Maybe I'll hang around here for a while." Adam got off his bike and sat down next to Mollie.

"See you, guys," I called over my shoulder, as I started toward the rock. Halfway there, my feet stopped walking. I wanted to run back to Mollie and Adam. You have to meet Laurel, I told myself. Just do it.

Now what? I couldn't believe it, Laurel wasn't waiting for me at the rock. Maybe she chickened out. I leaned against a maple and told myself, If she doesn't get here by the time I count to one hundred, I'm leaving. Laurel showed up at fifty-nine. She didn't even say hi to me. She said, "Kovar, if you know what's good for you, tell your mom to forget Thanksgiving."

I knew it. I was right. Laurel was faking it when she was being nice to Mom. It was all a big act. "No way!" I told her. "If you don't want to come for Thanksgiving, tell my mom yourself." I stuffed my hands into my jacket pockets. I didn't want Laurel to know my palms were sweating. She probably could hear my heart booming.

"Oh, my. Aren't we cool? Kovar, I have news for you. If you don't do something about Thanksgiving, I will. You don't want your mom to know about the tires, do you?"

"You're such a jerk, Laurel. What makes you think I won't tell your dad what you did?"

"Go ahead," Laurel laughed. "He knows."

"Well, for your information, my mom knows, too."

Laurel tossed back her hair. She didn't say anything for a minute. We both glared at each other. Laurel leaned against the rock. "Look," she said, "neither one of us wants our parents doing the

148

Brady Bunch rerun. We have to do something about it."

"No, we don't. My mom and your dad aren't doing a rerun of anything. They're just being themselves." I didn't know how I knew that. But I did. "So forget it," I said.

Laurel gave me the stare. I stared back. I wondered what she was going to say. I didn't think she'd start talking about Thanksgiving again, but she did. "Thanksgiving's no big deal, anyway," she said.

No big deal? What a switch. "What are you going to do?" I asked suspiciously.

"I'm going to call my mom. She'll probably want me to come to her wedding. So . . . I won't have to go to your house for Thanksgiving, anyway."

The way Laurel said it, I could tell she was faking again. Laurel knew she wasn't going to be with her mother. It was weird. I didn't know how I could feel sorry for Laurel Quigley. But I did. "If you don't . . . go to California, what are you going to do?" It would be worse than awful to eat a piece of pizza by yourself on Thanksgiving.

Laurel rubbed her finger back and forth across the rock. She didn't answer me.

"I bet your dad makes you come for dinner. My dad would." It was true. Daddy wouldn't want me or Jon or Mom to be alone on Thanksgiving. And Dr. Quigley wouldn't want Laurel to be alone, either. I knew he'd make her come. He made her come to our house on Halloween.

Laurel still didn't say anything. I wondered what she was thinking. I was thinking, Thanksgiving will be different this year. Dr. Quigley, Adam, and Laurel will be at our house for dinner. But so will Aunt Monica and Uncle Kevin. Jon and I won't fight. Mom won't be in bed with a headache. We'll have turkey instead of pizza. Aunt Monica will bring a pumpkin pie. Beth will probably come over after dinner. Maybe we'll play Scrabble.

"Hey," I said to Laurel, "it won't be as bad as you think. We'll probably have a Scrabble tournament. Jon always plays his guitar and we're going to have turkey, stuffing, and sweet potatoes for dinner."

"I hate sweet potatoes."

"You haven't tried my mom's."

Laurel shrugged.

"See ya," I said. I walked away from the rock.

I knew Mollie was waiting for me, and I was sure Adam would still be hanging around. I think I'll ask Mollie to come over to my house for brownies—maybe I'll ask Adam, too.

Sometimes you can really surprise yourself.